THE CHEATERS

Also by Ledru Baker, Jr.

And Be My Love
Brute Madness

THE CHEATERS

LEDRU BAKER, JR.

CUTTING EDGE

ISBN-13: 978-1-952138-59-1

Published by
Cutting Edge Books
PO Box 8212
Calabasas, CA 91372
www.cuttingedgebooks.com

TO MY WIFE, TRUDY

CHAPTER ONE

I STRUGGLED with the tie, managed a fair knot, and glared into the mirror. "What do you suppose Manny wants at this hour, Beanhead?" The reflection stared back, shrugged, and turned away as I reached for my hound's-tooth jacket. I felt a little too Vine Street, but the Boulevard was wearing them this year, and so was I.

Fifteen minutes later, I had bluffed my way through the afternoon eastbound traffic and was standing in front of the Psyche Ballroom, looking up at the marquee.

JACK GRIFFITH AND HIS ORCHESTRA
NOW APPEARING NIGHTLY!

I looked to the right. There was my picture in the window, just like a bull in the Farmers' Journal. My lips were curved up enough to be interesting to the heifers.

Little old me was sitting right close to the top of the heap, every now and then looking down to kick some goof ball in the teeth. Get up there, and you've got a thousand knives looking for your back.

I smiled down at the platinum key that the management had given me, slid it into the lock, and opened the door. I walked inside, down the plushly carpeted foyer that would have looked at home in a mortuary, echoed across the dance floor, and bowed at the vacant dance stand. My feet turned to the left and trotted up a flight of stairs to Manny Lewis' office. I rapped and walked inside.

The room was all drapery and leather, paneled in mahogany, sure of itself, and yet discreet, like a men's club. The lighting was indirect like an old maid's leer, and there was a friendly bar at the end of the room. Manny was there, and he guiltily downed the last of his drink when he saw me.

"Cocktail hour so early, Manny? You'll get the habit that way."

He jerked his fat head toward the bottles. "Build one, Jack."

"Not me, I'm still half in bed. What's the big deal?"

He turned back to the bar, poured two straight shots, and handed me a dollar's worth of Old Grand-Dad. "Drink it! I'm still boss here—for the rest of the day, anyhow."

I got cold inside for a long second, then tried a smile that died at birth. "Is it good and sharp, Manny?"

"Whatcha mean?" He scowled. He knew.

"I mean the ax. I've seen you soften 'em up for the kill before. Your routine's always the same: a drink, a friendly pat between the third and fourth ribs, just over the heart, and a smoke."

"Jack! You know me!"

"Sure, just a little too well, Manny. All right, get it over with. Now!"

He looked warm and embarrassed, but for him with his five-foot seven, two hundred and thirty pounds, it wasn't any trick. He took off his horn-rimmed glasses and polished them on the tail of his gawdy-bawdy sport shirt. He looked for all the world like a Melrose Avenue moneylender getting set to foreclose on a shoestring producer.

"Ever met Moss Morrison, Jack?"

"Yeah, once through his private army. You mean that little god's going to slip it to me personally?"

Manny's wriggly-piggly eyes jerked nervously around the room as if he was searching for a tape recorder. "Don't *ever* say that!" he cried.

"Oh, he'd squash me like a nasty bug?"

"No, but you'd never play again."

"Yeah. I heard last week that a cop got busted back to the Skid Row beat because he gave Moss's chauffeur a ticket. Damn it, Manny, quit playing cat-and-mouse. I don't have a hole to hide in this season. What does he want with me?"

"A divorce!"

"So he can marry me? I know it's stupid to ask, but why doesn't he get one?"

"Maybe he can't. No grounds."

"I'm crying deep inside. So what?"

Manny took a deep breath and tried to stare me down. I didn't stare down very well, and he finally gave up. "So you're going to help him get the grounds."

My mouth dropped open. With sheer muscular effort I brought it back from the driveling-idiot stage and tried to laugh. But it bubbled on my lips. It doesn't matter a damn who you are. When Moss Morrison, top dog in the syndicate, tells you to jump, you say, "How high, Mr. Morrison?"

And you don't come down till he says to.

I turned toward the bar, picked up the drink, and threw it into my mouth. The bar's mirror reflected my suddenly gray features, and the two of us stared at each other. The image said quietly, "Get guts, man, tell him to go to hell!" My silent reply came back: "Guts? I don't even know how to spell the word!" The mirror sneered and told me that I was a scared, yellow-bellied orchestra leader. I nodded in agreement and turned back to Manny.

"So what am I supposed to do, shack up with his wife in front of the newsreel cameras and vice squad?"

"That depends on what Moss decides, Jack."

Suddenly I was damned angry. I wasn't seeing only purple; the entire spectrum danced before my eyes. I grabbed Manny by the front of his shirt, twisted, and pulled upward. He came up on his toes like Nijinsky, his eyes wide and his face tight with surprise.

3

"You crazy little bastard!" I snarled down at him. "Who the hell do you think you're talking to? I may look like a damned fool, but I've got a long way to travel before I make your league!"

Almost gently he took my hand away, got down from his little pink toes, and tried vainly to smooth out the wrinkles in his silk shirt. He walked to the desk, creaked backward in the protesting swivel chair, and smiled up at me. The grimace would have looked good on Judas.

"It's all been arranged. He's gonna pay ya ten grand."

"Knock off that gangster line. This isn't Cicero, it's Sunset Boulevard, Hollywood, U.S.A. Talk American. Ten thousand isn't anything to what I'd lose in self-respect. I've got damned little of that stuff left, and it's got to last me for a few more years."

"You can buy a lot of anything for ten—"

"A lot of career, maybe? Who the devil would hire me after my so-called face got spread out all over the papers, not to mention my guts on the bedspread? Jealous husband—home-breaking orchestra leader—dirty bastard!"

Manny leaned across the desk. His eyes were pleading, shiny things, and his forehead was damp, even though the office was air-conditioned.

"You got to!" he said hoarsely. "It's my neck along with yours!"

"I thought you were in the syndicate, Manny. The word says that you joined up back in 1943 along with your beer-barrel dollars. Aren't you in charge of the dance halls? Haven't you got a percentage of the receipts in the other rackets?"

He shrugged, and his fat shoulders rippled up onto his neck. "I could be dealt out any time Moss Morrison didn't like my work. You might as well know that he don't like me, and is lookin' fer an excuse to—"

I put up my hand to quiet him down to a roar. "Wait a second! There's something here that doesn't sound quite right. I don't know what it is, but I've got news for you. I'm not going to be bottom dog in a gang fight. How come out of all this nasty world you picked on me?"

"Maybe because his wife has a crush on you."

"A *crush!* Well, why the blazes doesn't she come to my apartment and have it out with me? I've uncrushed a lot of women with my fumbling technique!"

"Probably because Moss is a good deal, and she doesn't want to lose him." He shrugged.

"How come you know so much about her?"

"We're good friends, in spite of Moss," he said. "She tells me a lot."

"So you pass it on to Moss when you can help yourself. Boy! You really believe in buttering the old bread, don't you?" He grunted and looked past me.

I nodded slowly just like the sinner who's received his eternal sentence. "So I'm in the middle, just like a piece of corned beef!"

"With mustard yet. Well, how about it?"

"What do you think, Simple Sampson? No. I won't do it!"

Manny sighed deeply, and maybe I heard a little sadness in it. "O.K., then, Jack. You're through here."

"*Through!* I've got a contract, you joker. As long as the gross take doesn't fall, you *can't* throw me out!"

He shook his head and reached into the center drawer, where a blank contract form lay waiting coyly. Yeah, and I knew what was coming: the fine print on the last page, the out for Moss Morrison.

Manny looked at me over the top of his executive glasses, the papers crackled in his hands, and he said, "Look. First off, I like you. You're not artistic like most of these bums."

"Yeah, I love you, too. Let's go steady with each other."

"Did you ever read all of your contract?"

"No. I was booked through the agency, and you know that there's not one musician in ten who can read anything but notes.

Go on, you sad sack, spill it. Then I'll take my beef to the musician's union."

"That's no good. Moss—"

"So you think he controls the union, too, just like your soul? That's great. Then I'll take up voodoo and stick pins in his effigy, and don't tell me he bosses the devil!"

Manny grunted and flipped through the sheets till he caught up with his pudgy finger and said, "Here it is, listen hard. 'If at any time the party of the second part so conducts himself as to bring discredit upon the party of the first part, the contract is immediately voidable upon the option of—"

"I know!" I yelled. "The party of the first part, the bastard. Now comes the gimmick. Did I make a couple of high-school girls?"

His voice was low, confidential, like a syndicate report. "Jack, we could prove that you made passes at half the women who came in here. We could get them to swear that you tried to make them in the middle of the floor during intermission."

"And charged extra admission, yet!" My face wasn't pretty, but then, neither were my thoughts. "Manny, you son-of-a-bitch, you're throwing it at me just to save your own greasy skin! What the hell kind of a buddy are you?"

He leaned forward, and his eyes were friendly. "Honest, now, do you blame me, Jack?"

I started to pour a drink, changed my mind, and sat on his shiny, glass-topped desk. If God had been listening to my prayers at that moment, the glass would have shattered into a thousand slivers, and one of the sharpest ones would have pierced Manny's heart.

"Guess not, Manny, but it's sure as hell dirty pool."

"The whole entertainment racket is," he said morosely. "If the mammas and daddys knew, they wouldn't let Junior come here to dance. Well, what say?"

"I say—no! I'll get out of here and get my boys another engagement. I was getting tired of—"

"Of three grand a week, a third of it take-home pay? Don't kid me, boy. This is Manny. We took you in here and made you. A year ago you were nobody."

"That's right, and a year from next hog-killin' time, I may be nobody again, but I've got to shave every day, and have to look myself in the face. Get yourself another boy, Manny."

"You'll never play anywhere else. You're *through*. I'll spell it out for you."

"Don't bother. I graduated from reform school, too. So I'll never play? Great! Then I'll get an organ grinder and take you along as the monkey. Better yet, I'll take my boat and get out of this whole lousy racket."

I got up and started from the office, suddenly tired of the whole thing. Get an orchestra together, create a style that's just enough different from the others so you'll stand out, kiss boots and other things to get a few records cut, pay through the nose for everything you get, sweat it out, pay salaries when you're going hungry and wish to God you had stayed where you once were, working for a living. Then make good! Yeah, get up on top of the heap, sit down, gather your coattails about you, and let them take pot shots at you. You, too, can make good. The life can't be beat. Nuts!

"Keep the old chin up, Manny."

"Sit down, Prima Donna," he said softly.

"We're all talked out. There aren't any words left, Fat Boy."

His voice was suddenly harsh. "*Sit down!*"

In spite of myself, I tossed my six-feet-something into a chair and tried to look around at my reflection for a bit of comfort. But I decided against it. It would be disgusted at having a namby-pamby for its owner, and ignore me.

"Moss will be here any minute. He said three o'clock, and he's always on time. You gotta tell him yourself."

"Is that in my contract? I have to explain why I won't frame his wife?"

"I take orders from Moss. He's the boss."

"Moss is the boss, huh? Hell, Manny, you're a poet. Are you going to keep me here?"

"Uh-uh, but you're stayin'. Maybe you like me a little. I sign the checks."

"Yeah, up to today you were all right, but now you're nothing but a sleazy little—Got any more reasons why I shouldn't push in your face and leave?"

"If you go now, Moss'll be mad."

"You mean he'll love me after I tell him he's a bastard?"

"Have a drink. You'll need it."

"So they're going to rough me up! Well, shove those drinks where they'll do the most good. I've got to like a man before I drink his liquor!"

Manny sighed and larded his way to the bar. He poured two more drinks and placed one in front of me. I reached for it, remembered who owned it, and pulled back my hand just as the door opened.

There wasn't any doubt as to who it was. Manny jumped to the position of attention and waltzed around the desk. His smile belonged on a puppy dog.

"Mr. Morrison, please come in!"

I turned around slowly. Like panzer divisions leading an attack, his guards advanced. Suddenly they parted, flanked me, and covered every section of the room. The man and legend Moss Morrison saw my staring look and smiled just enough to show that he didn't mind a cat looking at the king.

Liquor lobby in Sacramento, prostitution up and down the state, dope in Beverly hills, gambling in Los Angeles and eight clubs on the strip, bookmaking and wire services, three clubs in Las Vegas with three different front men, and God knows what else.

He waited for me to speak, but I was a dog if I was going to be the first one. Finally, with a gentle shrug to show that he didn't have any hard feelings, he spoke.

"How are you, Mr. Griffith?"

"Fine, thanks, Mr. Morrison."

My brave eyes hated him, at the same time admiring his poise. He was on the downgrade from forty and dressed to perfection. He was fairly tall, and it was easy to see that his dark blue business suit had less shoulder padding than the average. His face was good; it could have collected offerings at the Little Church around the Corner. His eyes were calm and gentle, and his silver hair made him look like a widow's dream.

He spoke again. "Has Manny told you, Mr. Griffith?"

"Yeah," I breathed. "He told me."

"And your answer?"

"You know what it is, or you wouldn't have asked me." I looked around at each of the scowling gorillas. "I'll tell you more when we can talk without these vultures listening in. They make me think of nothing less than sudden death."

His eyes crinkled; they liked me. The number-one dog leaned toward him and whispered. Morrison hesitated, then shook his head. Number One didn't like it and started to protest, then shrugged and turned back to me.

I grinned up into his sour face. "What's the matter, Rover, 'fraid I've got a Roscoe tucked away in my panties? Don't be afraid, Patsy, I won't hurt your meal ticket."

The screw head started toward me, then, like a good dog, stopped and heeled at a curt word from Moss. His face told me that he would like to work me over and make me a Believer. My eyes spoke back and said they'd like to see him try.

Trouble was, Man Mountain could have done it.

Morrison spoke softly to his men and moved his head toward the door. They left silently, unwillingly. The door shut behind them, and their nervous feet scuffled back and forth over the hall carpet. Morrison stood next to me, tall and straight.

"Well, Mr. Griffith?"

I took a deep breath and started to reach for the whisky, changed my mind, and stood up. His face was as expressionless as a tombstone.

"No!"

"Why not?" He was surprised at hearing that word for the first time since the year one, and showed it. But he bore up well and waited for me to speak again.

"I don't like frames."

"Neither do I, usually, but I think this one is justified. My wife and I haven't lived together for over a year."

"I get it. If a wife doesn't like beddy-bye fun, off with her head!"

"It isn't that. She's trying to drain me, and I don't like being played for a fool."

For some reason I looked at Manny. His face was as bland as unseasoned mashed potatoes. Then I looked back at Morrison. "No man does, Mr. Morrison, and that's my objection to the whole stinking idea. I'm not a Manny Lewis, I pick my own playmates."

Manny looked hurt and walked toward Mecca. "The usual, Mr. Morrison?"

Morrison looked genial and nodded. He was trying to be friendly, a man's man, whatever that is. Manny brought the drinks, one for him and the other for the big boss. He nodded at my untouched drink, and I silently ignored him.

Morrison stood, his drink poised. "Won't you join us, Mr. Griffith?"

"Thanks, I'll sit this one out."

The man Morrison took his whisky neat with no chaser, and I liked him for it. The liquor I had already drunk was starting its gay work, and I felt a little brave.

"Do me a favor, Mr. Morrison."

"Of course, Mr. Griffith."

"Drop that 'Mister' routine. You're paying my wages."

He laughed. We both sat down and looked at each other. Moss turned to Manny and smiled.

"Would you mind stepping out?" he asked softly.

Manny smiled happily, as if he was glad to get rid of the entire thing. His neck hung by a slender thread, and he loved that thread to payday and back. The door shut silently, Manny joined the animal parade in the hall, and Moss Morrison and I were alone.

In spite of myself, I was beginning to like Morrison, but that way lay serfdom, and I wasn't in the market for a slave yoke, size sixteen and a half. I scowled, fished for a cigarette, and offered him one when he pulled out his solid-gold lighter. We smoked in silence, a couple of old buddies. Then I spoke.

"For the next few minutes, you and I are equals. Sure, I'll admit that you could call your boys in here and have them work me over. But that wouldn't prove anything except that you can afford a bigger payroll than I can. And besides, it'd get blood all over Manny's carpet and upset the little beaver. Let's talk like men. O.K.?"

He grinned, and his teeth were straight, white, and all his own. "O.K. I like you, Jack."

"Maybe I like you, too. I only know what I read in the papers and hear on the Boulevard, and I don't believe much of that. Now, look. Why in the hell do you want to get rid of your wife? What's the real reason? Remember, now, maybe we're friends, so I want the straight scoop."

He leaned over and spoke quietly.

"She's a drunk. I never see her but what she has a drink in her hand. I like to drink, too, but I don't let it run my life. For breakfast, she has coffee with whisky. For dinner, she has whisky with coffee. I'm tired of the whole thing. Then, too, more than a little, I think she's a Lesbian."

I grinned. "Maybe you're a little too much for her."

He managed a smile. It was a weak thing, but he kept a man's leer out of it. "You may be right. We haven't got along together for a long time." He sighed and seemed to be trying to recall the last time he had been invited in. His lips moved, and he might have been saying her name. I felt sorry for him. I leaned forward and picked up the liquor. Its surface bobbed and winked at me; I lowered my winking eye at it and raised it to my dry lips. Maybe I didn't hate him, after all, and besides, I could use a drink.

"I've got a little question that maybe you won't like, but I'm curious."

"Let's hear it, Jack."

"Why don't you either buy her off or make her sort of—well, disappear?"

His face got masklike, and he tipped his head back to drink. I watched his throat muscles, and they didn't tighten at all when the liquor hit them. He placed the glass carefully down and said:

"She won't sell, and I don't kill."

"You mean—any more."

"Maybe—any more."

He walked to the bar, poured two more drinks, and returned. He handed me another good dollar's worth of Old Grand-Dad and sat down again. He crossed his legs casually and didn't seem to care about the creases.

"Do me a favor, Jack. Go look her up. Her name is Mardi." He said the word as it were all the poetry in the world.

"Nice name. Different. I might do that, Moss, and then again I might not. Where does she go?"

"To the Would You? Café on Vermont."

"Where the third sex hangs out?"

He felt bad, and his suddenly tight face showed it. The guy was in love with her, and he couldn't hide it.

"Then what, Moss? If you're the man I think you are, you won't like the idea of my playing with the woman you—*once* loved, even if you could get a divorce with the evidence."

His face was pained. "It's the only way I can deal with her. We'll talk about it later."

"You've had her followed?"

"Of course, but there was never anything—with men. She's left the place with women, but ..."

"You don't know what she did, and it's driving you nuts. I hear she has a crush on me."

"She plays your singing records by the hour."

"I've been told I sing like a bull moose during mating season."

He smiled faintly. "Who are we to disagree with the patrons of the Psyche Ballroom? They pay the tariff."

"Why haven't I ever seen her?"

"She built you up so that she's afraid of you."

"I hear she and Manny are pals. Did he tell you about it, too?"

Moss nodded. "He suggested your name, knowing how Mardi felt."

"The little bastard!" I laughed. "It's a funny thing to have a woman afraid of me. Tell you what, Moss ..."

"What's that, Maestro?"

Our grins liked each other. "I'll take a look. You've got me interested. Now get this: I won't help you to frame her, but anyone who's got the sense to like me must have something on the ball. I'll check things over."

"That's good enough for a start."

"I hear you'll break me if I don't play catch-wife."

"Maybe Manny put it a little too strongly, or maybe I would have before I met you. I don't see enough people who talk up to me; most of them are busy agreeing with me, hating my insides at the same time. You look things over. If you don't like the setup, we'll forget the whole matter. What do you say?"

"I'll buy it. And now you can buy me another drink this one's dying." I shuddered at that word and tilted my head back to drink.

CHAPTER TWO

WHEN I GOT outside again I turned the corner and walked toward Hollywood Boulevard, leaving my car parked on the street in front of the Psyche. My brain was working overtime every step of the way. For me, that was a new angle, and when I reached the Frolic Room my head was reeling and I needed a drink. Alex was there, as usual, ignoring the blatant talk that slid across the bar and dropped to the floor. He was at the near end of the bar, his feet propped on the chair, plotting the races.

He barely glanced up when I entered. He grunted. "I don't like that beast in the sixth, but my wife had a dream last night. She wants me to bet him. Last month I booked one of her bets myself that didn't even have an outside chance. It cost me a hundred and a quarter." He took off his new Hollywood horn-rimmed glasses and polished them carefully, giving me plenty of time to notice them.

"Goin' Hollywood, Alex?"

He sighted through them, blew a speck of tissue off, and grinned. "All gone, brother. I spot phonies better with this pair. The usual?"

I nodded, and he went to work on a drink, all gin, little vermouth, and a couple of ice cubes. They call it a very dry Martini, but it never gives you a head the next day. You don't have any left.

I leaned forward to sip from the sweating glass. Alex went back to his paper, and for a while I listened to the tall stories. You really shouldn't call them lies; they're just defense mechanisms the boys use in place of salaries between option pickups.

After two drinks, I went south on Vine Street to the Brown Derby Hollywood and got around one of the Meat Institute's better filets. Then more or less sober and satisfied, I strolled back to the Psyche Ballroom. The boys would be there by now; it was nearly seven-thirty. I wondered if Herbie would be in shape. He always came in at the last minute, flushed from walking off his daily jag. That damned weed has ruined more of my boys than I can count. They're good for a while, then it loses its kick and the needle takes over. Then look out!

When I told them I was taking a few days off, my boys crowded about me, saying they hoped I would be back soon, at least two of them praying that I would drop dead when I crossed the dance floor.

I explained that my nerves were on edge—doctor's advice—possible ulcer.

I wanted Moss to like me. I'd hit the big-time circuit just long enough to love the taste, and I didn't really want to give a straight no. The grind to the top had taken a long time. Although an all-American boy with gleaming white teeth would have told him to go to hell, I didn't feel very manly when I thought of eighty-two-fifty in a stinking refinery laboratory, working the graveyard shift the rest of my life. Before I got rolling with my music, I'd spent five years working in a lab, and it was for the little birds that hop on the pavement, picking up bits of things to eat.

Besides, it was work.

I took three parking tickets from my windshield and filed them with the others under the front seat. As I drove to the Would You? Café, I realized that I would have to move in and out—and fast; my arranger wouldn't take very long to slash me up and down, steal my best boys, and form his own orchestra.

In my pocket was a photograph that Moss had given me. If I'd been Moss, I would have clawed the bed and snapped at the mattress if she had denied me love. I would have gone a long way to keep her all mine.

Her mouth was the sort that sulked in a good-natured way, and her lower lip was the articulate kind that said, "C'mon, Baby, teach me something new—if you can!" Yeah, they got me, and the bold eyes backed up what I had suspected: She might be all he said she was, drunk, frigid, Lesbian, you name it. But whatever she was, her own story would be worth hearing.

I was lucky that night, and as I parked directly in front of the Would You?, I wondered if it foretold of great events like white arms and red lips. I moved in and sat at the bar near the door. The latest word from the private detectives had been that, as usual, she was here. And so here I was, too, my heart pounding more than usual, and my glands working overtime. I felt like a punk kid getting ready to move in on his favorite night-dream girl.

It was dark inside, lit only with purple lights. Booths were placed around the room, scattered with care, and the sides were tall. But they didn't really need to be; in a place like this, people minded their own business, and there was a minimum of table hopping.

The bartender was a nance. He was dressed in black satin; the blouse was clinging. His hair was blond and long, encased in a shimmering hair net. He wore lipstick with all the trimmings, powder, rouge, and mascara, all topped off with a couple of star-shaped beauty marks.

I liked him because he took my order without beating his false eyelashes to shreds. When I asked for a Martini, very dry, he gave me just that, with only a wave of the dry vermouth over the mixing glass. He took my money, looked at me closely to make sure he wasn't passing up any bets, then moved down the bar. The quarter tip I placed on the lacy napkin looked over at him, and quietly prayed that he would use it for a better grade of mascara.

I lifted the drink and looked around the room.

Then I saw her. She was sitting with a girl.

So what's wrong if she likes girls? I like them, too.

I sat watching her. In the flesh, she beat the picture all hollow, because she lived and breathed vitality. She was watching the girl closely, listening and nodding occasionally.

Through three more drinks I watched her, then her eyes raised and smacked into mine. They held on, bewildered at first, then a little afraid when she thought she recognized me. Then they grew bolder as she saw that I found her gorgeous. She leaned toward the other woman, her eyes still fastened on mine, whispered something, and half motioned toward me. I lowered my eyes as all good men will do at the right time, and finished my Martini in a quick gulp. I placed the glass down and looked at my hands. They were clammy, and my heart was beating all over my chest.

The next time I looked up, she was studying her drink, alone. At the far end of the bar, her friend had called the bartender, pulled gently on his curls, and was talking into his ear. Several times they both looked at me, and guess who they were talking about? Who else but Jack Griffith, the Sunset Stud?

The girl returned to the booth. Presently the bartender fished his way toward me, trying to look casual, like a cherry in a Manhattan. I helped him along by crooking my flirting finger at him.

He bounced up eagerly. "Yes, sir?"

"Could you make another one, just like the others?"

He was almost ecstatic. "Did you like them?"

"More than you'll ever know. Best ones I've tasted in years!"

He smiled happily, put a drop of vermouth in the mixing glass, and poured it half full of gin. He swirled it twice, dropped two olives in my glass, and poured the drink.

He set the remainder on the bar. "There's a little more when you're ready." He leaned forward, and his "Different Night" perfume smelled sweet till I remembered that he was a man.

"Don't let on I told you. There's a woman here who finds you interesting."

I looked slowly down the bar, on past two Lesbians talking earnestly with a young girl, farther on past the five-piece orchestra that was just assembling, into the booth where she sat alone, like a queen waiting for her king. Her companion hovered sulkingly on the outskirts, her hands rigid at her sides. She was watching my actions closely, and would have liked to see me dead.

I turned back to the bartender. "Who is she?"

He shrugged. "One of our regular customers. I never heard her name. She wants to meet you."

"I don't get it. She's with a dyke, and I'm a woman-lover."

He brushed his hair back and grinned. "I hate you! Don't worry about the dyke, she's not getting anywhere. A few queer women who like men come in here. You know, lots of enduring friendships were made at the Would You? Café."

"I'll *bet* there were! Say, what's your name?"

"Cecil. Cecil Riggs. What's yours?"

"Jack Griffith."

His eyes opened wider, and his lids fluttered just a little before he got them back under control. "I thought it was you. Your orchestra is at the Psyche, isn't it?"

"That's right. I'm taking a few days off before I drop dead and embarrass everyone. Something wrong with my guts, I guess."

He leaned closer, suddenly serious. "Why did you come in here, Jack?"

"Not for girls, or boys, Cecil. I just happened to see the place and came in. I'd heard about it from the fellows on the Boulevard, and got curious. Tell me, is she someone's doll?"

He wore his primness well. "I wouldn't know. You'll have to ask her."

I slid from the stool. The orchestra had been playing for several torrid minutes and finally segued from a brassy member into slinky *"Frenesi."* Couples were clinging together. Expensive slacks and short hair-do's were the vogue, and long glances were in order as hormones started gushing. I accidentally brushed one of them, got a hostile look, and finally stood by the booth. It had been the longest twenty feet I had ever walked. Moss's wife sat looking up at me like a startled doe in mating season. I leaned down. Her eyes stayed on mine, and her hand seemed to be trembling.

"I don't sell brushes for a living, but I'd like to sell myself for a drink. Are you buying?"

She started to speak, then picked up her glass and drained it. Taking it for an invitation, I slid into the booth. The Lesbian walked over and grasped my shoulder, working on a sensitive nerve as she squeezed. It hurt like hell as her muscular fingers dug deeper.

"Hadn't you better go back to your seat before I call the manager?" she said. Her voice was low.

"Manager?" I asked. "*I* manage things here."

I reached up, dug her claws from my shoulder, and twisted her arm backward till her face tensed and her lips clamped together. I let loose, and while she stood rubbing it, I said, "I'll leave when the lady asks me to." I turned back to Beautiful Dreamer, who was watching us, her lovely eyes wide with fright. "Shall I leave, miss?"

"No. That is, you may stay. I'll buy us a drink. All *three* of us," she said, turning to the girl.

Gruff Voice started to slide into the booth, but I put my hand against her chest. "Get yourself another doll for the evening. This one's taken." Her thin lips curled back over irregular teeth, and I went on. "One word out of you, and I'll have you yanked in for impersonation. You don't fool me. You're a man!"

The ugly thing she used for a mouth dropped open in time with my new friend's. She stood for a long minute, leaning on the booth, breathing hard, and hating me with each jerky breath. At last she drew herself erect and left. She was so mad that she'd be taking up with men next.

"Miss, maybe I played it a little rough," I said, "but I wanted to talk with you. Don't ask me why, I'm just built that way. I see a girl and do things. I lose a lot of teeth, but it's fun."

The orchestra blared up, then settled back to passion strains. "It's all right. I guess I wanted to meet you, too," she whispered.

"Maybe our friendship won't last long enough to make any difference, but my name's Jack."

"Jack! You *are* Jack Griffith!"

"Yes, whatever that means."

She sank back, and if I'd been singing at that moment, I swear she would have swooned.

I leaned forward. "What's the matter?"

"I've heard you sing!"

"I wave my hands, too, and smile at the audience. Have you seen me do that?"

"I've never seen you before. I—I …"

"Aye, yi, yi, yi!" I sang. "It's beginning to sound like a Mexican dance. All right, you're one up on me. What's *your* name?"

"Mardi. Mardi Morrison."

Drop dead, Moss, and let me take over. I'll love you for it, and I'll set up a perpetual shrine at your grave!

The waitress came up with the drinks; I felt gay and laughing inside and wanted to pat her fanny till I realized that she was a he. I turned back to Mardi.

I felt like the original peeping Tom who was looking at the loveliest woman in the world. When she spoke, she had the maddening habit of running a pink tongue over her already moist lips, making them shine even more in the purple light. She was slowly driving me mad, and I counted Moss Morrison out for the original fool. I'd have given anything to be alone with her.

"I like you, Mardi!" I said suddenly. She leaned forward, and the high-necked blouse seemed ashamed of itself for hiding her body.

"I like you, too, Jack."

"Let's dance."

"Let's." she murmured.

We weaved into the maze of dancers, one of the few mixed couples on the floor. She slid into my arms. Her eyes were soft against mine.

Her body molded itself into mine, and we were like one body doing an eternal dance of love and all that goes with it. As in a dream, the dance was perfect. We drew nearer till our lips were almost touching. Once her tongue stabbed out and almost felt my mouth. She sighed and closed her eyes as my hand went lower on her hips and drew her even closer to me. Her breasts were crushed against my chest, and I said to myself, Get a hold on yourself, lad. You've had it!

When the dance was over, we returned to the booth. I took a drink, scowled, grubbed for a cigarette, and said:

"Would you like to go somewhere and ... Look, don't get me wrong, but I ... Forget it," I ended.

"But you—what?" She leaned toward me and her tender breasts were poised things above the table, questioning me silently. I looked back to her eyes, and they were eager now. I tried to look away, but they followed and brought my eyes back, smack into hers.

"Finish what you were going to say!"

"Damn it, Mardi, I don't *know* what I was going to say!"

But I did know one thing: If we left, Moss's detectives would follow us, and I wasn't buying a double cross that night. Thanks a lot, but no, thanks, Moss. However, I wanted to be alone with her and talk, know more about her, kiss her mouth and hold her hand, hear her secrets and become part of her dreams.

I looked across the table at her honey hair and gorgeous eyes, her sultry smile and full lips. Then I looked down and saw her rings for the first time. The engagement stone was an emerald-cut diamond that could have ransomed the national debt—pre-Truman era. I frowned and didn't know quite what to say when she raised her eyes to mine and softly asked:

"Didn't you know I was married?"

"I should've guessed it, a woman like you."

"A woman like me?" she breathed.

"Yeah. You're not bad-looking."

"Maybe you're all right, too."

"Could be. I haven't asked my agent lately."

"Do you want to hear about my husband?"

I was suddenly gruff, using the all-man technique. "It's none of my business. Skip it!"

She looked hurt, and I felt like the original bastard. "I just thought maybe you'd like to know. I'm sorry."

"Maybe I know too much already."

Things went on like that through three or four more drinks. I studied her as she drank, and she didn't look like a candidate for Alcoholics Anonymous. She drank slowly, only when I did, and didn't gulp them down like a confirmed drunkard drinking for escape.

When I had drunk enough, it seemed natural to lean forward over the beating rhythm of the music and whisper, "Kiss me, Mardi!"

Without hesitation she leaned forward and gave me her mouth. Life was born that instant under her clinging lips. They worked against mine and said hello in the ageless manner. Her sharp teeth caught my lower lip and bit. I loved the sharp pain, and my tongue felt the cut flesh and bragged a little.

She wilted against the table. Her hands sought mine and gripped them tightly. All the clocks in the world stopped moving. Our lips parted reluctantly, clung together for one more eternal instant when I leaned toward her, then separated. The devil could have been watching for all I would have cared.

Or God, because it was that wonderful and holy.

Or Moss Morrison, and I would have spat at him and flown to the moon with Mardi.

She spoke first. "Let's leave, Jack."

Just like that. And what did I say to her? "Let's leave, Mardi."

We left the café arm in arm, and Moss's detectives could have been snapping pictures for all their little warped fingers were worth for all I cared. I had heaven on my arm and a soft, warm smell lingered in my nostrils. We got in my car. She turned willingly to me, and her arms were open and warm.

"Wait, Mardi. Let's get off this street."

I wheeled the car from the curb, screeched across the tracks, turned onto Santa Monica Boulevard, then north on the first dark street. No one followed us. The car rocked to a halt. I killed the engine and turned to her.

"I'll take that kiss now."

She swung around slowly till she was lying across my lap. Her arms slid around my neck, and she pulled my head down to hers. Her lips were alive under mine; no one had ever been kissed like that before.

Her body arched, begging for my hands, and made its every curve mine. Her fingers pressed me tightly against her, and I memorized every moment, because I knew there would be no more.

Because I had to sit up, look into her lovely face, and say:

"Your husband wants me to frame you!"

There was no slap across the face, no bitter, obscene curses, no nothing. She merely sat up, fixed her blouse, and said softly, "Thanks for telling me so nicely."

I lit a cigarette and scowled into its fresh ember. "Shall I take you home?"

"Maybe you'd better."

I switched on the ignition, turned it off, and threw the cigarette into the darkness. It arced away, and I watched the embers die on the black asphalt. I started to light another one, then threw the entire package away. I turned to her and put my arm on her shoulders.

"Just a minute ago, I was in heaven. Now the devil could have me without a fight."

She nodded. "I know what you mean."

"I wonder if you do. Mardi, I could love you from here to hell and back. Do you believe me?"

"We're both drunk!" she said harshly. "But maybe there are some things *I* could tell *you*."

"Listen! I've been with lots of women, drunk *and* sober, but I never said that before tonight."

"I told my husband that a long time ago."

"But did you mean it?"

"I don't know. Maybe I loved him a little."

"What happened between you two? Forget it," I mumbled. "Tell me it's none of my business."

"I don't mind. He's nice enough, as men go."

"Is that why you hang out at the Would You? Café?"

"That might be the reason, only I don't 'hang out' there. I just go there to be with people who're as mixed up as I am."

"What about that girl tonight?"

"Louise? She's all right, but I—we haven't…" She stumbled with the words.

"I don't have the right to ask, but have you ever…"

She looked at me, and even through the darkness of the car I could see that her eyes were honest. "No. Never!"

"What about your husband, then?"

"If I loved him, it would be different. But knowing what he is, I can't stand to have him touch me! Do you believe me?"

"I think so, my dear."

"I never kissed him like I just kissed you."

"Because you were drunk tonight, maybe?"

She looked hurt, the way women will when a man agrees with them.

"I'm asking things that I haven't bought the right to, but I've got to know."

"Go ahead."

"Why don't you give him a divorce?"

"I don't quite know. I'm all mixed up, I tell you."

"What if he *sued* you for divorce?"

"I couldn't stop him if he did, but he won't—never! He's worried that I'll fight him some way."

"He's *afraid* of you?"

"Yes. Forget it. It's not your problem."

"Maybe it is, a little. Do you remember how you kissed me?"

"How could I forget it?" She turned her face away and looked into a dark house. I couldn't help but wonder in how many dark houses people were making love.

"And how I kissed you?"

"Yes."

"Maybe, like you said, we were both drunk, but I don't believe it."

She reached out in a little nervous gesture. "It's no good, Jack. Forget the whole thing; I beg you to. Please! Now, will you take me home?"

"After you say one thing, if you mean it."

She leaned toward me, her sweetness wafting with her. It was more than just perfume, something I can't understand and that's impossible to explain. Her lips moved slowly toward mine, and my mouth stayed motionless until it wouldn't wait any longer. It swooped down on her, falcon-like. My arms went out, and our bodies were tightly pressed together.

My mouth told her everything it could in that kiss. Hers silently answered back. Then the kiss was over, and our eyes met.

"I love you, Mardi!"

Her mouth came forward again and kissed me. My thoughts retreated, my eyes closed, and I said to myself:

This is it, boy. Good luck!

CHAPTER THREE

THE GRAY MORNING was a funeral shroud that hung over Sunset Boulevard, hiding the mourners that picked their ways along. I pushed myself out of the bed, felt my way to the kitchen, and brewed an acrid pot of coffee. While it ripened, I leaned against the sink and had fingernails for breakfast as slowly the memories of the past night returned to me. Right down to the last scene in front of her Sunset Boulevard mansion, I hated myself, and if someone had called for his dog right then, I'd have got down on all fours and barked.

The coffee was erupting in the pot, spilling on the stove, but it still wasn't bitter enough for me.

The phone's muffled tone shattered through the apartment like an angry snake's rattle. I snarled at the begging coffee and went to answer the phone. Even after I picked up the receiver, I didn't speak, because the memory of that last kiss flooded back to me. She was in my arms again, her fingers pressing me tightly, her mouth alive under mine.

"*Hello!*" It was a woman's voice, strong and nasal. She brought me back with a bang, and I resented it.

"Hello. Who is it?"

"Mr. Griffith? One moment, this is Mr. Morrison's office."

The hair on my neck raised, and my muscles started to twitch. Moss, I was only kidding. I only gave her a little kiss—or two!

But his voice was athletic dub, strong and friendly, and I realized then that if he had a bone to pick with me, he'd send his army over.

"Hi, Jack, this is Moss."

Shoot the works. You've got nothing to lose, kid!

"Hi, Moss. I like your wife."

He drew in his breath, and was as surprised as I was. Then he laughed.

"What can I do for you this murderous morning?" I said.

As if I didn't know!

"How about lunch, Jack?"

"Sure. Where and what time?"

"The Baroness' at one?"

"I hope to God you're paying! That phony European harridan charges more for her eight-course meal than I clear in a month."

He laughed again. "I'll take the meal off my non-reportable income tax that I don't pay."

He was still chuckling as I replaced the receiver. I apologized to the snarling coffee, had two cups, unrawed a couple of eggs, burned some bread, showered, shaved, then went to see my piano.

Usually when I'm low, my buddy Steinway helps me. I give him free rein, and he talks back to me, lots of times giving me the answers I need—or want, maybe. My fingers roamed over the keyboard, idly, like that joker who lost the chord. Yeah, something was lost, all right, and as I sat listening, I realized what it was.

My heart.

My nervous hands crashed onto the keys, and music came out, music that I hadn't thought of for years: Hungarian Rhapsody Number Two, by Liszt. My eyes were closed as the composition played itself, and I was with Mardi in far-off royal Hungary.

Then with three crashing chords it was over, and I sat looking down at my fingers, which were suddenly whiter than the keys. The woman was afraid of something, and one guess would tell you what. She knew too much about Moss Morrison, and yet, slicing it against the grain, he was afraid of her. God, what a family, all sweetness and light and mutual trust! Why should he be afraid of any woman? As sure as municipal graft, if any woman got close to where he lived—his secrets—wife or no wife, he would have her taken care of. Don't give me that line, Moss. You'd kill your own mother if she knew too much!

And then as I sat, watching my fingers relax as the blood flowed back into the tips, I knew why he didn't turn magician and have her disappear.

He couldn't. She was too smart for that; he was under her well-manicured little thumb. Then it slammed me between the eyes. He didn't especially want a divorce. I, Jack Griffith (The Music You Love to Dance To), was his own, freshly hired trigger boy!

He expected me to find out how much she knew, and where it was hidden besides her pretty little brain. Step up, step up! You too can make good. Get on Moss's bandwagon. Take care of Moss, and he'll take care of you!

Four-letter word twice in rapid succession, then slam down your hands and make a violent discord on the keys.

I don't like the hand, Moss. You dealt it from a cold deck. Let's have another deal, and this time *I'll* break the seal and shuffle the cards. I got up to dress for my luncheon engagement with my new buddy, Moss Morrison, Mr. Big of Racket Town, number one in the graft parade.

The Baroness', where the elite meet to sneer and trade wives. And if you're in the inner circle, maybe the Baroness will invite you into her private office for a drink—alone. She's notorious. They say that she knows more about the arts of love than even Cleopatra dreamed up with all her slaves.

There's no place like it. And the women patrons, oo-la-la! But magnificent, *mon ami*. They're owned by rich men, every one of them, as long as you don't count the few who go there to be seen by rich men who are tired of owning women like them.

The Baroness. The woman's a genius!

I loved the headwaiter, because he let me in without a struggle and refused the bill I had folded discreetly in my hand. In the booth I sat, drinking my Martini, the best in the world for a dollar and a quarter.

Across the room in another booth a lovely rich bitch sat. She made it look like a bed with her warm presence and worked her breasts for me several times just to show that she had them under control. I flexed my profile for her. She took out a cigarette and put it between her expensive lips. She started searching for a match, and I was getting ready to motion the waiter over to help her out when Moss came into the room.

Hail Caesar!

Not until he was standing next to the booth did I realize that he might be waiting for me to recognize him and get homage ready. I throttled the natural impulse to jump up, and instead said:

"Hi, Moss. Drop it and join me in the Baroness' private rotgut."

The headwaiter scowled down. I curled my lips just enough to show my canines, and he advanced, maybe even a little humbly.

Moss sat down. "A double shot with water, please."

He grinned. I had come in prepared to hate him, but somehow I couldn't. We sat looking at each other while the waiter brought the drink.

Moss raised his glass. "Luck, Jack!"

"I'll be needing it."

He finished his drink and motioned for another round, then brought out a platinum cigarette case, studied the cigarette situation, and offered me one. We puffed for a few seconds, and I waited for what I knew was coming. He eased the ash off into a cut-glass ash tray and said casually: "So you liked my wife?"

I prickled beneath his inscrutable stare, and answered, "She's all right."

"I mean, did you get along?"

"We got along, but not that way."

"You left in a hurry. What happened?"

Yeah, what *did* happen? Who went ahead and kissed a woman, then like a congenital idiot all but swore eternal love?

When I looked back at Moss, my face was as transparent as cellophane on a package of cigarettes. Try the truth on for size, Jackie; it won't hurt much.

"I just wanted to be alone with her."

"She got you. Right?"

"Yeah, right in between the left and right ventricles. She's all right, and for God's sake, don't tell me she gets 'em all that way!"

He raised a steady, understanding hand. "She never tried to. As far as I know, she never cheated on me—with men."

"I've got big news for you, Moss. She hasn't with women, either." He looked sharply at me, to be sure he was getting the straight copy. I nodded. "That's right. As far as I know, she hasn't chippied with anyone—including me. Does that make you feel better?"

The lines around his mouth smoothed out, and he nodded slowly. "You'll never know." He watched his cigarette, which lay smoldering in the tray. The smoke spiraled upward and sought the invisible air-conditioning unit.

"But don't be too sure of anything, Moss. It's a rare husband who's sure of his wife. I've got lots of friends who lost theirs by trusting too much."

"A wife you can pick up any day."

"But you can't drop one so quickly, can you? Look, Moss, you're playing a game without telling me all the rules."

His patrician eyebrows raised; he didn't seem to get it, so I tried again. "We both know that you could get a divorce. Even without my help you could frame her. But you're not doing that, and I want to know why. If I'm going to play on your team, I want to know what rules we're using—Marquis of Queensbury, or East Side blackjack."

He didn't like what he heard, and his majestic features suddenly developed a fissure. "Don't ever play on *my* team and try to change sides!"

"As long as the rules are fair, I won't. Now, here comes the question of the day: Why did you pick me? I mean, just whose idea was it? All Manny's, or partly your wife's?"

He stopped to think. "Manny's. I knew he was telling the truth about her liking you, because she played your records a lot. Then he told me that you might be willing to do it, if the right way was used."

"The little bastard used the right approach, there's no doubt about that. Work with Moss, or die! That was what it amounted to. And I didn't like it, not worth a damn. So they're good friends, huh?"

He raised his hand. "Nothing like sex, I'm sure of it."

I grunted. The drinks came, and we both watched them, then lifted them and drank. "By the way, Moss, where's Murder, Incorporated?"

He smiled. "Outside, waiting."

"What the devil are you afraid of, Moss? Those goons don't love you, and if they got a better offer, they'd dump you in the river before you could say concrete overcoat."

He nodded again. He was very agreeable today.

"Moss, have you read the papers lately? You know this Flossie Narbonne, don't you? She's making you the laughingstock of our L.A. Why not drop those hopped-up apes and start living? How long has it been since you went someplace with only your conscience to pester you?"

His smile didn't come off too well. "Too many people want me dead," he said simply.

I leaned forward and put my arm on his sleeve. "See what I just did? I touched you because I like you. If I tried that with your men around, they'd kill me dead. Moss! People, whoever they are, don't go around knocking other people off in broad daylight.

That takes a police permit, and I've sort of gathered that you've got the cops sewed up in your tailor-made vest pocket. Your enemies will wait till you're alone, like poor little Bugsy, sitting in your house, reading the Wall Street Journal, or in bed …. Say! Do your boys go to bed with you?"

He laughed. "They sleep on the floor at the foot of the bed."

"Well, it's none of my business, anyway. But I think you know I'm right. Now—do I get a good answer, or do I leave you and take up with Blonde Beauty across the way? She might like a playtime cruise in my cabin cruiser."

His laughter reached across the room to Dream Dish. She half looked at us, arched her back so that her breasts could see us better, and wet her lips so they would shine more in the subdued light. Moss looked at her, then back at me.

"I recognized her five minutes ago, Jack. She's from one of my better houses on Wilshire. This must be her free day. We give them hunting time."

"Well, anyway, let's have the story, Moss."

He played with the dead cigarette, then dropped it and looked up at me. His eyes were more honest than a seminary student's. "If she'll divorce me, she can have a quarter of a million dollars."

"With no strings?"

He hesitated, tallied up the score so far, then said, "That's right."

"I've got something to say, buddy."

"Shoot—buddy!" His smile was colder than the outside of my glass.

I finished my drink in a rapid gulp and said, "I'm going to marry your wife."

"Marry Mardi!" His look was unbelieving until my open, truthful eyes swore that they spoke the truth.

"Do you mean that?" His voice was hard, but caught somewhere in it was surprise, and maybe even a little fear.

"Sure, or I wouldn't have said it."

"Do you—think you love her?"

"If I didn't, would I be sticking out this scrawny neck of mine? Yes, I *do!* But get this, I'm not aiming for any shakedown. If she leaves you, there won't be any of that dowry money. Not one penny!"

He leaned back and studied the frescoed ceiling as if he were an engineer. I could almost hear the wheels going around in his brain, trying to come up with a good answer. It's not every husband who has another man propose to him for his wife's hand. I was beginning to enjoy the scene and looked across the room at Glamour Stuff. I lowered my winking eye and leered wickedly when she smiled and waited for more. I turned back to Moss.

"Well, if she'll have me, can I marry her? The way things stand now, she's not doing either of us any good."

His voice was low, and into it crept the reason why he was Mr. Big. "It's not that easy. I can't afford to let her go."

"So your bluff wasn't any good, was it, Moss?"

"Don't get too sharp!" he warned.

"Sharp, hell!" I cried. The girl looked across at me, alarmed, and I lowered my voice. "You tried to sell me a lousy piece of goods, and I didn't buy it. Now you tell me to go dig myself a hole. I've got some more news for you; I'm not hibernating this season. I didn't want to get in this mess, but you and your boy Manny dragged me into it. And now that I'm in it, you suddenly want me out. It's not that easy. I met your wife, and if she'll have me, I'll take over where you left off and furnish the bread and butter for our table."

His hand came over and gripped my arm. I tried to shrug it off, but it clung too tightly. The eyes that stabbed into mine belonged to a stranger.

"You're out, as of now!"

"Nuts!" I grinned. "I'm in it as much as I ever was. Why weren't you the man I thought you were? Why didn't you come out and tell me what you really wanted? What swami told you that I was a congenital idiot?"

That was a lot of questions. His hand dropped off, and I sank back and waited for his answers. He remained silent as the moon, and as far away.

"Why didn't you tell me you wanted something on her so you could be in a better bargaining position? You can't fool me the way you can the others. I'm not afraid of you, and for some fool reason, I won't ever be." His face would have shamed a frozen Daiquiri as he watched and listened. I arose slowly. "Eat by yourself, and the drinks are on you."

"I'm not through talking," he said quietly.

"Well, *I'm* through, Buster Boy. I don't like my hand, and I'm picking up what few chips I have left. I could have liked you, but you're not playing the game my way."

"There's only one way to play this game."

"Yeah, and that's your way. No, thanks. That leads to the silent grave, and I'm not ready for that trip. So long!"

"You'll never get out of here!" he warned scowlingly.

"You'll bet on that? I've got fifty bucks that says I'm at Wilshire Boulevard in five minutes. As you were, chum!" I said. He started to get up. I placed my hand on the front of his double-breasted suit and pushed. He thumped back on the seat and stared up at me, not quite able to believe that anyone had touched him.

I could feel his eyes watch me as I walked slowly from the dining room into the bar. Once past the bar, I made time down the plush-lined gin mill, past two doors marked in French for boys and girls, turned left, opened a door marked "Private" over a phony European coat of arms, and cut into an office.

The Baroness didn't expect a visitor, but I didn't care, and the blush that came on my cheeks had to do with the technique, not the act. I simpered my way through the room before the Baroness, a chic, graying woman, and her lover, an aging juvenile, could jump up from the position of love. I started whistling a ribald tune the Baroness would understand, bowed as I walked, tipped an imaginary hat, and went through the rear door into the alley.

Wilshire Boulevard sprawled along less than a block away. With my back twitching, I made it and hopped the local bus for Hollywood. As the traffic flowed by, it reminded me of how my own career had folded, how it would soon be a thing of the dead past, a musty something that I could remember when I humbly knocked on the gates of the refinery and went back to work as a laboratory inspector.

I would never play again. Moss (just call me God for short) would see to that. But then as we passed Western Avenue, and I saw two couples in a hot rod, laughing and singing, I didn't really care any more. I just wanted to get away from the entire stinking mess, somewhere out on the ocean in my boat, completely removed from the entertainment racket.

I even promised myself that I would throw my Hallicrafter two-way radio to the fish and leave civilization forever. I never wanted to hear any kind of music again, and during the next lifetime, if any Christmas carolers came across my path, I'd lay a horse whip across their ecstatic shoulders.

Damn, I hated people! Including myself.

CHAPTER FOUR

I STOOD by the open window in my apartment, looking down over the sprawling city that was slowly dying in the dusk. On the horizon, storm clouds were piling up, and a towering thunderhead was slowly moving in over the city, its trailing tail following like an angry rudder. The sun went down suddenly as if God had pulled a curtain across the sky, and the wind rose, flapping the drapes in the room. A few pelts of icy rain slammed against my face, but I stood there, barely feeling them.

With a drink in one hand and my pipe in the other, I looked like a man of distinction, only I was drinking the wrong liquor, my hair wasn't graying at the temples, and I wasn't feeling very distinguished.

Look down on the city. Write a song, a thousand songs. Call them all "My City."

Make it like Gordon Jenkins' "Manhattan Towers." Start out with the piano as solo, resounding chords. "My City! You're all about me from the dark hills above to the glittering boulevards beneath. From the magnificent clubs on the Strip to the smoke-filled dives on Central Avenue." Yeah, write a thousand songs, start them out with thundering movements, each one with a deep sob hidden in the chords. Then ripple along to show the flash and speed of Hollywood. Drop back a little and pick up the heartache and pathos that belong there, then speed ahead again, but be sure that when the song is through you've shown hope and triumph. Ya gotta do that. That's box-office, and ya can't make a living with just plain art!

I remembered back over the years when I first came to my city, and how within two whirlwind years I had made good. Without even knifing anyone, either. They moved me from my Normandie Avenue hovel to here. But I had liked it over there, and resisted. I had credit at the liquor store and bar, but *they* were unhappy with my living there. "They" were Manny Lewis, the hangers-on, and the girls. "It just won't do, my dear. You're up there now, and you *must* live correctly. Get your things together. I'll get a suitable apartment and speak to a decorator I know. He's nothing less than a dream!"

So here I was, twenty-eight years old, a going-down-and-outer, sliding down the ladder on the seat of my expensive doe-skin slacks.

Damn Moss Morrison!

Curse Manny Lewis!

Yeah, and to hell with Mardi!

I was spoiled-fish sick. There'll be no more big money for you, my lad. You're headed back to hamburger, not even ground round. There'll be no more fine meals at the Rocking Horse Grill on Restaurant Row.

Back to the grind. You'll never play again!

I was getting drunk, but that was good; the sharpness of my emotions was gradually losing its edge. The bottle and glass clinked together in my unsteady hands, and for a second, my guardian angel let me look ahead ten years. There was a stumbling bum, shuffling his way along to the blood-donor place on Skid Row. His lips moved soundlessly, and his mind was intent on one thing: to give his begging stomach a gallon of wine. He traded his blood for four dollars, almost fainted when the bright sunlight hit him, and headed for the liquor store on Third Street. I felt sorry for him, then saw my face on his bent shoulders.

I shuddered, put the liquor down, and felt my way to the bathroom. Under a cold shower, my own personal brand of determination returned, and I commenced making plans. How much could I carry away from the wreckage? Maybe eight thousand dollars if I could dump the lease on someone. And the orchestra was no problem. That son-of-a-bitching arranger Tommy Smith could have them. I chuckled. Whatcha suppose he'll change his name to, Jack? Something commercial like "Jennings Randolph and His Purloined Dozen."

After a fashion, I dried off and flopped on the king-size bed. The decorator would have gone wild at seeing me on the satin coverlet, making big wrinkles out of little ones. I tossed and turned, thinking of Mardi.

Mardi, where did you get that body, and how did you bewitch me? Your mouth—did you ever stop to think how lucky you are to be able to kiss the inside of it every minute of the day? You can caress your body. Lord, I'd love to spend a day, watching you unobserved, loving your face when it relaxed, bringing my mouth to yours, unseen and unfelt, and brushing it lightly with mine.

Sleep was for someone else, it was a pool of quicksilver, and at seven o'clock I arose, a little wobbly, but stone-cold sober. I'd make it, all right. I left my car at home, got a cruising cab, and went to work.

"Back for good, Jack?" The doorman grinned at me when he helped me out of the cab.

"For good or bad, I'm back—for tonight, Bill. I've got to pick up a few pallbearers. Want to sign up on the waiting list?"

He was worried. "Is it *that* bad?"

"Naw, I'm just kidding. Is Manny here yet?"

"Yeah, he came in 'bout an hour ago, mad about something. He almost chewed my head off. Just for nothing, too."

"Forget it. These are trying times for all of us. How's the gate?"

"Just fair, but it's early yet. It'll pick up."

"Yeah. S'long, Bill."

"Take care of yourself, Jack."

I swung around the dance floor, past the seats with their little two-drink-size tables, on to the long, curving bar, waved to the bartender, and shook my head when he held a bottle temptingly high. As I neared Manny's office, my guts got colder. I almost changed my mind about that drink.

Through the closed door, I could hear Manny talking to someone, most of the time grunting Indian-like in a monotone. I tried not to listen, and walked a few feet away, then came back when I figured he would be finished. His voice was wound up like an alarm clock, and finally he screamed:

"All right, I hope to God you know the score. Yeah, yeah, I got it in the mail today, eight cents due. Goddamn it, sure I'm nervous." There was more listening, then Manny grunted again. "Sure I'm gonna. What the hell would you two do if I didn't? O.K., good-by!"

He slammed the phone down. After a couple of seconds I knocked and walked inside. He was sliding a clip in what looked like a .38 automatic and jerked his head up nervously when I entered. He fumbled with the gun as if it were suddenly white-hot, then dropped it in the drawer. His face was livid with rage as he yelled, "Why the hell don'tcha knock?"

"I did, then I came in. You never told me to be formal before. What's the gat for—got the payroll in here?"

He inhaled deeply and walked to the bar. He tossed a quick drink down without offering me one, then remembered and jerked his head toward the bar. "Build one. And forget what you saw." He grinned, but it would have looked better on a three-day-old corpse.

"I'm mum, you know that." I made a drink and walked over to him. "Well, what about tonight, Manny?"

"What *about* it?"

"You know damned well what I mean! Did you get any orders from Moss?"

He tried to look as if he had forgotten. "Yeah, you're through here. We're givin' you two weeks' extra pay."

"Just so I'll leave like a good boy with no harsh words. Well, you take that money and ... No, better yet, make a check payable to the Salvation Army. I'll probably be their prize case inside of a year. O.K., I'm leaving. 'By!"

He was suddenly jittery like spit on a hot stove. "Do me a favor, huh, Jack?"

"Probably not. What is it?"

"Stick around a few minutes. Go down to the bar and I'll meet you there. I want you to say so long to the fellows; they all like you. After all ..." His shrug was eloquent, and I understood.

Yeah, after all, I had to. I had no fight with the first sax or the second bartender. And you don't bow out of two years' existence with not even a good-by wave.

"All right, I'll go down and say good-by, but you don't need to come. I'd feel better if we were alone." Below, I heard the boys shuffle chairs around on the stand and start tuning up. I wondered if Herbie was on time. "Be seein' you, Manny. Say hello to Moss. Tell him I'll see him—someday."

He looked at me for a long time, and I thought he was going to say something deathless, philosophical, maybe, but he just grunted and said, "No hard feelin's, Jack?"

"Hell, no, none at all, Manny. I'd do the same to you." I shook hands with him to show I didn't really mind walking out on a good job and left the room.

I went down the stairs, hands in pockets, and stopped to look over the place. A few people were eating on the far side, and bits of laughter floated across to me. Some more customers were drinking at the bar, and just then three couples strolled in, gaily expectant. I got to feeling dramatic as all outdoors and realized that never again would I have a moment like this. Then I got an itch and scratched it. I grinned. Good God, can't I ever have my moment without spoiling it? I started whistling and trotted down the stairs.

At the bar, my favorite stool snuggled around my fanny. I waited for the bartender, Ulysses S. Hobart, to walk over. He had been polishing a glass; he put it behind the bar and lit a cigarette after offering me one. He poured himself a straight shot, looked carefully around, then wiped it to his lips. It made a fast blur and he grinned.

"Neat trick!" I complimented him.

He grinned. "Thanks, podner. What'll it be tonight?"

"A double Martini, and drop the vermouth, more or less. Let's call it gin on the rocks."

"I call it double death. Not working tonight?"

"Nope. I'm through."

"He really did you in, huh?"

"What do *you* know about it?"

He started working on my drink. "Not much, Jack, except the word's out that you're poison on account of having a fight with Moss Morrison. It's funny how things like that get out, isn't it?"

"Yeah, funny like a funeral. Maybe you hadn't better be seen talking with a has-been."

"If I didn't think you were kiddin', I'd slug you, Jack."

"Sure, I'm the world's best kidder. Join me in one last drink, Ulysses?"

He roared and several patrons looked around disapprovingly at the noise. "What the hell do you think I made the mixing glass chock-full for? What the hell, it isn't every day I lose a friend."

"Thanks, friend," I said.

He poured the glasses, raised his, and looked me in the eye. "Don't do anything nutty, Jack. No job's worth it."

"I won't."

A customer sat down and coughed for service. Ulysses started taking care of him, and I swiveled around and watched the orchestra. On the stand, Smith was leaning over, quietly giving poor Herbie hell. Herbie was trying to ignore him and was crooning softly to his drums. He was still on the jag, he was to blame, but Smith wasn't handling it right.

God help the fellows who tie up with him, I thought. He's got a Caesar complex, and his slaves will lead a rugged life. The Martini was getting a good start at digesting my stomach lining when the music started, the theme song that I had written years ago: "How Did You Know?"

For several bars the piano carried the theme solo, then the saxes took over, moaned and died away, leaving the trombones to wail. The music softened at an imperial wave of Smith's hand, and he went to the microphone.

"Good evening, ladies and gentlemen. This is your host, Tom Smith, taking over where Jack Griffith left off. Jack is still ailing, but we hope to have him back with us soon."

Oh, God, did you hear that lie!

"And now, here's a brand-spankin' new ditty, written by yours truly, Tommy Smith, called 'Sunshine.' Hope you like it!"

My stomach rebelled as the music started. I shoved it back in place, but it said, "To hell with it, boss, I'm coming up again." I soothed it with another swallow, and smiled sadly. That song was one that I had composed a month ago. I had turned it over to Smith for arranging. He had tied a new handle on it and called it his own.

The pirate!

And then suddenly it wasn't important. Nothing was important except to get out of town. From my apartment, I could call Mardi, and she would immediately understand why I wanted to be alone. She was the only one I could talk with.

I turned back to the bar. I brought the drink to my lips when ...

"Hello, Jack."

The voice was soft and low; in mythology it had belonged to a siren.

"Mardi!"

CHAPTER FIVE

WHEELED ABOUT, and she advanced slowly toward me, walking like a queen. She was wearing dark glasses and a long-sleeved evening dress. She smiled and sat next to me. Her presence was warm and necessary like the beating of my heart. I reached over to remove her glasses, but she drew back.

"Practicing to be a movie star, Mardi?"

She looked hurt. "My eyes were just tired."

"Mine are that way from looking at you for just ten seconds."

"Am I that bad?" She smiled, knowing what my answer would be.

"You're that gorgeous, and you know it."

I leaned forward to kiss her cheek and saw a dark bruise. I jerked the glasses from her face, and her arm flew up.

"No, Jack. No!"

"The dirty bastard!" I cried. "Picking on women at his age."

I gently replaced the glasses, cupped her chin in my hand, and steered her lovely face toward mine. She winced in pain.

"When did it happen?"

"This afternoon."

"I'll kill the dog!" I cried.

Several near-by drinkers looked curiously at me, memorized the hatred on my face, then turned back to buzz. Ulysses came up and stood waiting, his worried eyes fixed on Mardi's face. I turned to him.

"Two more Martinis, Ulysses. Double, huh?"

He shook his head sadly and bent over to mix the drinks. Mardi put her hand on my arm, and it was like a shock of high voltage.

"Jack, I want you to promise me something."

"I know, forgive and forget. But I'm not built that way."

"Don't do anything. Please tell me you won't!"

"What kind of a man do you think I am? Of course I will!"

"No!" she cried. "I'm—going to leave him. Tomorrow morning I'm flying to Reno for a divorce."

"You're sure?"

"Jack, were we drunk the other night?"

Her lips were close to mine, soft, and nothing less than wonderful. "What do you think, Mardi?"

"I had hoped not."

Ulysses reverently placed the drinks in front of us. I reached for my wallet, but he shook his head. He went back to polishing his glassware, now and then turning his worried eyes toward us.

I lifted the drink. "Luck, Mardi!"

"Is that all? Just—luck?"

"What more can a friend say?"

"Just a friend?" she murmured.

"Look, doll, I'm down and out, in case Moss didn't tell you. He didn't like my stock and he sold me short. It's going to take a lot of sweat and blood to get another start. Maybe I will eventually, but it'll take a long time to give you the sort of life you're used to. Once upon a time I ate margarine, and now I'm going back to it, like most of the other citizens. Maybe you think I'm a fool, but I'm fighting mad, and I'm going to beat my way up again. It won't be music. Those days are past—Moss will see to that. But somehow I'm coming back. It's not only pride; I admit that I like the fancy things in life. I'd rather stay at the Beverly Wilshire than a beach motel.

"Here's what I'm trying to say: I'll be working hard. If you want to wait, God bless you, but I won't let our romance be spoiled by poverty and hard times. So that's it. Get your divorce and let me look you up later."

Hard to say?

Don't be a fool. It killed me. I saw two glistening tears roll down her cheeks. She buried her face in her hands and dry sobs came out. She tried to speak, and her body shook. I patted her shoulder. She drew her nerves together, repaired the break in them with make-up that she brought out of an overnight-type purse, then turned to face me. Her smile was as brittle as fine china.

She said. "I have to leave now."

"Where are you going?"

"I have to pick up some things at the house."

"I'll buy you clothes!"

She shook her head. "No, there are other things that I need, and I don't have the money to spend."

"Do you think I'd let you go back there? Baby, you don't know Jack very well. I'll loan you the money."

"No, I won't take any money from you!"

"Then—then I'll pick them up for you."

She was eagerly pathetic. "Would you? I hate to think of going back there."

I took a deep breath. "Sure. I'll go."

"Moss is still there, but he's leaving for Las Vegas at nine o'clock. Wait till, say, ten or ten-thirty."

I frowned. "Yeah, maybe it'd be better. If I saw him, I'd slug him, and his goons would kill me slightly."

"He fired them today. I don't know why, but they're gone."

I rubbed my chin, thinking back and wondering if what I had said had shamed him into his decision. Then I grinned and rubbed my hands together. She understood and shook her head.

"No, Jack, I won't let you go there till he's left for Vegas."

I grunted unhappily.

"Take me to your place while we wait, Jack? I'd like to see it once."

Her voice dragged me back from a very neat scene. I had Moss's throat in my hands and was banging his noble head on the floor. I jumped nervously and said, "Sure. Let's go."

Heavy clouds had lowered, re-formed, and were rolling in turbulent masses around the lights of downtown Hollywood. Rain was beginning to fall, and large drops hit us as we walked out. The air smelled electrically clean, like a lineful of washing, carrying with it a restless quality that made my neck hairs rise.

Bill whistled a cab over, helped us in, and refused the half dollar that I held out. I thought kindly of him, because it was an odds-on chance that I would be needing all the half dollars I could lay my hands on.

I gave the driver the address and settled back. The rain was coming down harder than ever, blinding things all around. Lightning flashed and thunder rolled down from the hills, cracking and bellowing above us like my own personal hell.

Mardi snuggled against me, and my arm went around her warmness. She shuddered as the thunder increased and lightning filled the sky with flame.

"Afraid of the storm?"

"Not especially. I just don't like it."

"Guess I know what you mean. A *perfect* night for a murder."

"Jack, for God's sake, don't say that!"

The cab had been creeping through the driving rain. Suddenly a new convertible, its top still down, whipped from the private section of the parking lot. Its horn blasted as it cut in front of us. The cabbie swore and slammed on his brakes, throwing us forward in the seat. The bright-yellow Cadillac careened onto Ivar and stopped at the signal. The top went forward as the hunched driver pressed the button.

The driver was bitter. "That crazy son of a—"

"Tut-tut," I interrupted. "It's all in a nighttime."

"The damned fool coulda wrecked my cab!"

"Your *cab!*" I roared. "What about your passengers?"

The man turned around to snarl. I slid my lips back over my teeth. He saw them gleaming in the darkness, grunted, and turned back to his driving. My teeth always gleam at night; it's a habit they picked up in Italy when I used to roam around inside the off-limits areas. More than once they've gleamed me out of trouble.

At that instant, I remembered who owned the Cadillac. Manny Lewis had plunked down heavy sugar just last month for it and had driven me around the block while I clucked my tongue approvingly. It was his, all right. I shrugged and looked at Mardi as the driver bounced out into the heavy traffic.

Mardi lifted her face to mine for a kiss, and I smiled down at her poised lips. "Later, baby, not in a cab. I'm a big boy now."

"Maybe it's now or never."

"That could be, but I'll bet it's later. What's a bet worth?"

She looked at me, and her eyes were the brightest things I had ever seen; they were like cat's eyes in the dark. "Maybe nothing," she whispered softly. "Or maybe a kiss. I'll think it over."

We got from the cab and ran into the apartment house. Inside the private elevator, I didn't even touch her, but when we entered my place, my arms went about her. The kiss had been worth waiting for. I thought of the king-size bed, then dropped my hands suddenly.

Take it easy, Jack. You've waited this long, and a few more weeks won't kill you. Go brew her a hot cup of tea.

CHAPTER SIX

WHILE I SLOPPED a few towels on the rain-soaked floor, Mardi walked through the place, like a conquering general inspecting a captured villa. I was kneeling down, working small puddles into large ones, when I felt her presence near me. I turned around, and she was standing in the middle of the room, her eyes watching me work.

I felt bold. I dropped the dripping towels on the floor and walked toward her. She backed away slowly, an inviting smile on her curved lips. She reached the divan, sank down on it, and waited for me. As I stood over her, a pair of inviting arms reached up, slowly moving, inviting me to join heaven. Her mouth was poised, like a velvet trap, and as I looked at her, I knew that she could have me forever.

I dropped slowly down. She drew away till she was reclining full length on the divan. Her breasts were violent things that strained against the silk of her dress. My eyes looked, and my lips were suddenly hungry. The dress was nothing, and my eager hands easily defeated it.

Then my lips rose to hers; life was worth living, and there was no retreating from anything. I couldn't help whispering to my soul, "Hold tight, you've just grabbed the brass ring!"

Her hands were gentle when they brought my head toward her mouth. She smiled a little and bit my lower lip. The pain was exquisite like that first night, something to be loved till days had no meaning, something to remember when the last breath is leaving. I pulled away, looked at her, then pushed myself up.

She leaned back, smiled sleepily, and ran long fingers down her body. She held out her arms to me and whispered, "Afraid of yourself?"

"Yep, and of you, too. I'm not old-fashioned, and if you were a one-night doll, I'd go ahead with my playtime routine. But you're not. I think I love you."

She arranged her dress. "I should kiss you for that, but I won't. It wasn't nice to get me all up in the air. 'Twasn't nice at all!"

"*You* up in the air!" I grinned. "What about me?" I got serious. "You know you wouldn't like it the way things stand now."

She looked me up and down. "Maybe just this once I would."

Like a fool, I turned away, went to the kitchen, and mixed a pair of Martinis. Minutes later we were sitting together on the divan, but with discreet inches between us.

Mardi reached into her purse and took out a golden key.

"This is for the front door, Jack."

I took it, turning it over, admiring its golden color. "Well, at least I won't have to go in through the service entrance. What does the iceman use, a common silver job?"

"I left my suitcase in the hallway, behind the flower stand at the head of the stairs. Bring it back here, and I'll let you drive me to the airport."

"That's big of you!" I grinned.

We drank instead of talking for the next several minutes. Then I spoke again. "What have you got on him, Mardi?"

She looked a little startled, then said, "Enough to put him away in prison for a long time, and perhaps cause his death— with the syndicate. Even though he is a senior member, they'd kill him if they thought he was cheating. It's a nasty business." Her shudder was genuine.

I placed the drink down. "You've got enough to buy yourself a neat little annuity, haven't you?"

Her eyes were twin Roman candles, and her hand flashed down toward my face. She stopped it in time, looked at me sadly, and shook her head. I hated myself and grubbed for a cigarette.

"Look, baby," I said, "I've been around a little. Not in the slick, fast, egg-sucking crowd that hangs around Moss, but just enough so I think I'm a pretty smart boy. I want you to tell me something, and so help me God, if you don't give me a straight answer, I'll walk out of here, and you'll never see me again."

"Don't say that!" she cried. Her face was white like the cliffs of Dover, and her skin was tightly drawn. "You can't leave me!"

"It's up to you. Just give me the straight word on one thing: Do you want to get rid of Moss?"

"*Yes!*"

The reply was blunt, but that was the way I wanted it, rather than an eventual shot in the back and a grave in a quick-lime pit.

I looked at her bruised face. "I believe you. Now, where's this creepy evidence of yours?"

She lit a cigarette and leaned back. Her eyes fixed themselves on mine. "Jack, more than anyone, you have a right to know. But I can't tell you. It's in a safe place. Let's leave it at that. For my own sake, I've got to be the only one who knows. You're a good citizen, and if I told you, you'd probably go out and get yourself killed trying to find it."

"Yeah. Number One Citizen, that's me. They pin badges on my chest every day. Just what is this syndicate? Like everyone who reads the Daily News and Times, I know about it, but what is it? Really, I mean."

Her eyes stared across the room at my original Julien painting of a Michigan spring scene. "After all the gang killings during prohibition, the boys got smart and divided the territories up among themselves, according to sections and states. They joined forces, made a sort of corporation for their own protection. That way, the public that supports them doesn't really know about what goes on underneath the surface. Generally it works out fine; anyone who wants to start up a racket—big-time stuff, that is—has to get a permit from the syndicate and cut them in, or the local law-enforcement departments will close them up."

"You mean that nearly all cops are crooked?"

"No, not that, but some of them are blind. They have to be to stay in office. It's all very businesslike. They even have directors' meetings and quarterly reports. But now and then, one of them gets an idea on how to chisel a little extra. Since most of the income isn't reportable to Internal Revenue, a certain amount of chiseling can be done. At any rate, that's what Moss has been doing, among other things that the F.B.I. would like to know."

"Where does Manny fit into the picture?"

She smiled. "Little Manny. I'll always like him, I guess. He came into the syndicate when times were rough, just before the war. During prohibition, he took five million dollars out of illegal breweries. I really don't know how, because he doesn't seem too smart, but he made it, and I guess that's the important thing. They let him in, with no voting rights, but a percentage cut of the net take."

"If he's in, then why is he so afraid of Moss?"

"In a way, Moss could kick him out tonight if he wanted to, although Manny is really the next man here."

"Let's slow down a minute. Supposing something happened to Manny. What would happen to his share of the profits and stock?"

"The money would go to his heirs. It's all very legal."

"Yeah, I can see that. Legal like hell."

"But now, Moss handles everything on the West Coast."

"From dope and gambling to prostitution and lobbying, huh? He's a brainy little cuss, isn't he? But I've got a question. Where'd you get the idea to check up on him? That isn't very wifely, is it?"

"I guess I was afraid of him. If he ever decided to get rid of me, I wanted to have something to hold over his head. A few weeks after we were married, I got the combination to his wall safe."

"Did he work you over when he caught you spying on him?"

"Not till today. I told him over a year ago that when I died, my papers were to be opened up. He knew what that meant."

"I'll bet he did. Does anyone else know about these papers?"

"No one but you."

"If he gives you a divorce, will you return them?"

She leaned toward me. When her long, silky hair brushed my face, she took it and wrapped the long strands around my neck, trapping me. Her breath was soft in my face. Then she asked me softly, "Would it make any difference to you?"

Her mouth opened and captured mine. The kiss was long and involved, containing wisdom from the pages of Giovanni Boccaccio to Walter Benton. She gave me every ampere she had in her body; when I tried to raise my arms, they were paralyzed, hanging numbly at my sides. My breath was a forgotten thing in my lungs. I swayed, then opened my eyes and saw her lazily smiling at me.

"It's time for you to go, Jack."

Time for me to *go*!

"Mardi, another kiss like that and I'll die. I swear I will!"

"Don't die now. You've got to go to my house."

"O.K. I won't be long." I took the rest of the drink in a gulp and barely felt it. My hands were trembling, and I shoved them into my pockets.

"All right, Jack. I'll wait here. Be careful. And remember—I love you!"

A hundred-dollar golden swallow held the address 9427 Sunset in its beak. The house loomed high and lonely above the curving lawn that rose from the Boulevard, like a proud king above his subjects. It was what they call an English colonial, I think, and looked colonial as all slavery.

When I got from my car, the rain had died, and the moon was rising above the eaves as if it worked for the place. But the storm clouds were closing in again, and darkness took over as the clouds boiled and fought for supremacy.

I parked on the street. I was worried. It isn't every day you go into a man's house to pick up his wife's bag so she can leave and marry you.

The wet grass squished and slithered beneath my feet, and the rain hit my face like an angry woman as it slanted down across the house. I should have used the driveway, but its crunching gravel would have made more noise than a three-minute commercial on a five-hundred-watt radio station. As I took the key from my pocket, my palm was sweating; I found the lock and piously, like a grave robber, swung the huge carved door open.

Any shadow I might have cast was swallowed up in the great darkness. I took the lighter from my pocket; it flared up and showed the curving stairway that rose majestically to the second floor. The lighter died, and I cursed myself for not filling it, as I felt my uncertain way across the dark room. Suddenly the breath died inside me, and I almost dropped to the floor.

A light shone out from under a door on my left. I stood, trying to build up nerve enough to go to the stairs. I thought of taking off my shoes, but realized how foolish I'd look if Moss saw me, peekabooing, shoes in hand.

I tiptoed toward the stairway. Then a sound made my nostrils clog up and my heart thump in my chest.

Someone groaned. It was a horrible sound, like the dead trying to get back to life. I walked closer to the door. There was another gurgle, then a sob. I got my guts up in a nice, tight little knot, put my hand on the doorknob, and prayed for a long second.

Then I flung the door open. The light blinded me, and my arm automatically went over my eyes. Then things got back to normal, and I looked around the medievally ornamented room, past the battle-axes, suits of armor, centuries-old original prints, and authentic skull drinking mugs, to the most hideous sight in the world. A dying man.

Moss was still breathing, but the gasps were costing him heavily and were precious things that he tried to save. He turned his head and looked across the room at me, stark terror in his eyes. He finally recognized me, and his hand rose a few inches and fell back, like a dead fish tied onto a dying man's arm. I ran across the room and knelt down beside him.

"Moss, for God's sake, what happened?"

He tried to speak, but the jibbering that came in front of the bright red blood didn't make any sense. He coughed, and the frothy bubbles exploded. I picked him up from the floor and sat him at the desk. The coughs came again, gushed onto the shiny glass, spread out like a lake, and filmed over. A dull object caught my eyes. I looked down on the floor next to the desk and saw the gun. I could have sworn that it was the gun I had seen Manny juggling in his office earlier that evening.

The blue smell of powder hung in the air like tobacco smoke, and Moss's labored breathing was hard on my ears. He made a warrior's valiant effort to sit up; he pushed himself from the desk, and my eyes saw the bloody hole in the heart side of his silk gown. Blood was pulsing out slowly, and he looked down at it unbelievingly.

He fell back in the chair like a tired executive and closed his eyes. The chair turned, and I reached over to grab him. He leaned toward me, then slumped sideways and toppled to the floor, his body making a hideously inanimate sound. I dropped down beside him, turned him over, and took his head in my arms. I knew from the war that more than any-thing a dying man wants company in his big moment. His eyes opened and looked into mine, and his blood-caked lips moved silently.

"Who did it, Moss?"

His voice was carved from the rough edge of a file. It was coarse, unbearable, but he got one word out.

"Manny."

He coughed in his hand and looked at the blood, then raised his pained eyes to mine. "Jack, I let my bodyguard go today like you said. Look what—it got me!"

His eyes brightened like a lamp about to go out, then they faded and two more words came out: "Mardi—love!"

He died hard, coughing blood from his lungs. But he made it, and took his last breath like a man. Over his body I made a vow that didn't make a lot of sense, but I meant it, tearful eyes, staring features, and all.

"I'll get him for you, Moss. I swear to God I will!" But the blank face and dead eyes didn't give a damn what I said. They didn't hear it.

A harsh voice slammed through the room. "Get up with your hands in front of you!"

I hadn't heard the door open, but the Policeman's Manual was behind me, undoubtedly with an aimed gun. I arose slowly and turned around. A revolver was pointed at my stomach. My head shook sadly at him, and tears formed in my eyes.

"Why'd you do it?" the hostile voice asked me.

I was astounded. "I didn't!" The figure stood in the shadows beneath a large ax. The starkness of the sharp edge fell on his face and made him look like an inquisitor from the great days of the rack and iron maiden. Another figure moved, and my eyes turned to the right. A uniformed cop stood by the door, eager and alert, a rookie straight from Poly High.

"Who are you?" the first voice asked.

My head shook dumbly, and I took a step toward him; it was a gesture of friendship that should have been molded from our shared intimacy with death. But his gun raised and pointed in my bewildered eyes.

"Stay where you are! What's your name?"

"Jack Griffith."

His look belonged on a network television show. It was wise and amused. "Oh, the song boy. Well, I'll be damned. I heard you had a fight with him, but I didn't think it would go this far. All right," he sighed. "Let's have your story. It's bound to be good."

My mouth tried a pitiful grin that wound up on the floor. "There isn't any story. I found him when he was dying."

"When he was dying!" He smiled, and his teeth were crooked and yellow from too much coal tar and cheap cigars. "Now," and his voice tried to get confidential, like a Boy Scout counseler, "tell me. Who did it, his tailor?" He turned toward the other cop, whose returning grin was weak and unsure.

My lips curled back like a cornered animal's. I could have murdered him, except that he had a police .38, snub-nosed and deadly as a hooded cobra. The other officer saw my nervous movements and slowly drew his gun.

"Naw, smart boy! Not his tailor. You've got me in a corner, so I'll tell you who. He said Manny Lewis killed him!"

His eyes narrowed; his breath caught, then came out in well-measured cadence. "Well, how convenient! Next time why don't you use Alice in Wonderland? It'll sound as good."

"Look, whoever you are, that's what he said. I've got nothing against Manny, but you've got me in a spot."

"Just a good friend of Manny's."

"I can afford to be. I'm not a cop."

"Police officer," he corrected almost gently. "Where's Morrison's wife?"

"In my apartment."

His eyes glittered, and in that moment he was the prosecuting attorney, judge, jury, and executioner all combined. "In your apartment! This is going to save the state a lot of money. What was she doing, reading the Rubaiyat of Omar Khayyam to you?"

"Don't be so sharp. I didn't have to tell you that."

"Maybe you did. Let's say someone saw you."

"No one saw us. I've got a private elevator. No operator."

He grunted, walked over to Moss's chilling body, and nudged it with his polished toe. "I always hate to see a dead man."

"Yeah, I know, it makes you want to cry!" His lips worked around like a tough guy's. I walked over to him till his gun got all official again. "As long as you're so worried about me, why don't you ask Manny Lewis a few questions? Try his alibi out for size."

He looked at me, his face twisted like a prize pretzel. "You're eager, Griffith. What's the answer? It smells like a tight frame."

"You're not going to pick him up?"

"Maybe. You found Morrison like this?"

"Oh, my God!" I moaned. "Here we go. No, I—"

The front door opened, footsteps echoed through the empty house, and all heads turned toward the study door. We all waited for something to happen. And it did. Manny walked into the room, his little lips pursed in a silent whistle. He saw us, and he came to a screeching halt. He seemed to sense that something was wrong, and he turned to each of our faces in turn.

The uniformed cop stepped backward at the first one's nod, the way they had taught him on page 49 of the Manual. My number-one enemy walked forward to Manny, trying to be a cop, but playing it safe at the same time.

"Hello, Manny."

"Hi, Grebel, I … Good God!" Manny cried when he saw the twisted, stiffening body. "Not—"

"Yeah, Manny," I said. "That's our boss there. Too bad you weren't here ten minutes ago. He was talking about you."

"Knock it off, Griffith!" the Grebel character warned. He turned to Manny, "Where were you earlier?"

"In my office."

"Why'd you come here?"

"Moss had heard—" Manny turned to me. "Look, Jack, nothing personal, but you know how it is."

"Sure, Manny," I said gently. "I'm beginning to get it."

Manny turned back to the master inquisitor. "Moss heard that Jack here was threatening him, and had been steppin' out with his wife at the same time. He asked me to come over and see what we could do about takin' care of him. Legally, that is," he finished hastily.

"Sure. Legal like murder, huh, Manny?" I asked. "Moss told me you—"

"Drop it, Griffith!" Grebel exploded. "I don't want to have to rough you up!"

"Rough me up!" I yelled. "Come to think of it, just what right *have* you to do that? I don't even think you're a cop."

"You don't have to, but here's my badge."

He held out a gold and silver badge. There was an identification picture in the wallet next to it.

"What department?" I asked.

He made a low stage bow. "I am Lieutenant Grebel of the Vice Squad, at your service."

"Isn't murder a little out of your territory?"

"No, Griffith, it isn't. I just finished raiding one of Mr. Morrison's houses, and I came by to see if he was here. I've been trying to connect him with the racket for months. I saw your car parked in front and came in. Something smelled bad."

I interrupted. "And now it smells even worse, Grebel."

"Why, Number One Suspect?"

"I've been around a little, and this starts to read like that nice tight little frame you were talking about. If you're going to play it that way, as a private citizen I demand that you arrest Manny Lewis as a suspect along with me. Let's make the knife cut both ways!"

"Jack, you tryin' to give me trouble?" Manny cried.

Grebel looked over his shoulder and called to the young and honest patrolman. "Johnson, take Mr. Griffith out in the hall. Now!" he roared when the bewildered cop moved slowly forward.

I looked at Grebel while the cop grabbed for my arm. Grebel was the sort you'd miss in a crowd, medium build, medium everything, except his eyes, and they were hard chunks of obsidian from the lava flows in the Mojave Desert. He was a dangerous man, and as his mocking eyes looked at me, I knew that he wouldn't run from anything, including a pay-off.

The G.I. cop said firmly. "Come with me!"

"Page one-hundred and eight of the Manual?" I asked. "How to make an efficient arrest."

"Go with him, and no trouble!" Grebel warned.

I held back a second, half jerking the cop from his feet. "Grebel, you're a lousy bastard."

His smile was thin like a scalpel. "I love you, too. Get him out, Johnson. Lose him, and it's your neck!"

In the hall, I paced back and forth, Johnson almost trotting to keep up with me. Finally he put his hand on my shoulder and skidded me to a stop; I forgot to signal, and we thumped together.

"Look, Mr. Griffith," he almost pleaded. "Don't make it hard on me. I don't want to cuff you, but I'm goin' to have to if you don't shape up. Now do me a favor and stand still."

I looked at him. "How long have you been on the force, Johnson?"

He almost blushed. "Two months."

"You'll learn." I looked toward the closed door. "Yeah, you'll get hep to a lot of angles if you stick with it. You're too honest, Johnson. You'll never make the team that way. Get smart with the boys, and you'll be off shift work with a desk and a nice fat graft roll for yourself."

"I didn't join the force for that. My brother was killed last year stopping a holdup."

I wanted to say something, like how Grebel was working with the very forces his brother died fighting, but it wouldn't have served any purpose except to make the cop feel bad. As it was, he felt noble, as if he was avenging his brother's death. He started to speak again, but the door opened and he popped to the position of attention. One hand dropped on my shoulder.

Grebel walked up, his smile cold. "All right, Griffith. Let's meander."

"Where?"

"To the station."

"Slip it gently, Grebel. What's the word?"

He shrugged his shoulders; the expensive suit rode up, then fell into its perfect folds again. "Let's just say—material witness."

"Don't twist it, Grebel. I'm a smart lad. Are you booking me?"

He was hurt and surprised, then he gave up the sham. "Yes. For suspicion of murder."

"Goddamn you!" I screamed. "What about Manny Lewis?"

"He couldn't have killed Mr. Morrison. They were good friends."

"Friends, huh? How come you know so much about Morrison, anyway? You *really* get around! Where's Manny now?"

"He left—through the study."

"Oh," I breathed gently. "I get the whole stinking setup. Brother, will *I* have some talking to do when I get down there!"

Grebel's face was suddenly next to mine, and in a sour whisper he breathed, *"When!"*

He turned to the cop. "The cuffs!" he muttered.

"The hell you say!" I yelled. "You're not slipping the noose around my neck. You know damned well I didn't kill Moss!"

The G.I. cop shook his head and fumbled for the handcuffs. Grebel stood watching me with a sardonic grin on his face. I looked toward the front door, back in the study, then over at Grebel.

"Go to hell. I'm sitting this one out!" I roared.

"Grab him!" Grebel screamed. I swung wildly at his jaw, and he staggered back, hitting his head on a chair as he fell. Before the astonished cop could raise his drooping jaw and flip open his holster, I bolted for the study and locked the door. I wheeled about, looking for Manny, saw the open French windows, and followed in Manny's murderous little footsteps. Just before I stepped out, I turned back for a pitying glance at Moss's body.

"I haven't forgotten, Moss!"

They were cursing and lunging against the door as I ran into the patio, crunched a few expensive tropical plants beneath my feet, and started running toward the front. I raced across the driveway onto the wet lawn. The expensive clover cursed as I dug my furtive toes into it for footing and started my race for life.

Just as I was getting a decent start, too many things happened. A car, probably Manny's, roared away from the curb, and behind me, a door opened. A shaft of light shot across the lawn, pinning me for an instant. Someone shouted and guns started firing at me.

Ever had anyone shoot at you? The sounds cracked out, and my running back cringed for the stunning blow. Many times the two men fired at my twisting path, but always I managed to zig when they zagged. I ran down the slight hill, bent my knees, and leaped over a five-foot hedge onto the wet sidewalk. I fell and slid, sprawling on my face.

There wasn't any pain as my knees and legs slammed into the cement; anger and fear were too powerful antidotes. I jumped up and crouchingly ran to the car, slid the key in the ignition, and pressed on the starter. I felt like kissing each and every piston and valve as the car purred. I took off, slid around the next corner west, and headed away from the battle grounds of Operation Frame-up.

Five minutes later, I had left the lights and was speeding southwest to Santa Monica. I hit the back streets, then curved southeast through the beach towns of Manhattan, Hermosa, and Redondo into the darkness of the Palos Verdes Hills toward San Pedro, my boat, and escape.

Damned fool?

Maybe, but who would I be kidding if I stayed there? It was for sure that Grebel never meant for me to get to the station. And even if I made it that far, that would only be the first of many roads that led north to San Quentin, and the gas chamber.

And Mardi would softly cry when she got the news of my execution.

And Manny and Grebel would grin and lift a toast to my chemically treated remains.

No, thanks, I'll play it my way.

Here goes nothing. Shoot the works!

CHAPTER SEVEN

THE RAIN slashed down in a deadly, impersonal manner as the wiper cursed and slopped its way back and forth over the curved windshield. Each round trip only meant more work, and I felt sorry for it. Tons of rain pounded down, blinding the road and closing in about me as if all the devils were in the storm clouds.

But I thanked God for it, including the weather man for good measure. I was cruising along at forty-five. I had passed through the little village of Palos Verdes and was sliding around curves, scarcely touching the brake. For the last ten minutes, there had been no other cars, and for a while I was safe. More or less.

I could guess what had gone on in that room.

"Well, Manny?"

"Yeah, Grebel?"

"Didja kill him?"

"*Me?*" Manny would be hurt at the thought. "Why should I knock off my boss?"

"People have done it before. It's goin' to take lots of explainin' when Griffith starts talking. The rest of the organization will hear about it. You're number two here, and you stand to move up a notch."

"Yeah. Ya know, Griffith might not *get* to the station. It could be that he'll try to escape."

"That'd be risky."

"Bought any insurance lately, Grebel?"

"On a cop's pay? You've got me laughing!"

"Why laugh? I've got a friend who sells insurance damned cheap. He could sign you up on a ten-grand policy."

"When does it get ripe?"

"When Griffith tries to escape."

"Maybe your friend's got a customer. But tell him to have the policy all ready. It makes me nervous to wait."

"It'll be there."

"O.K. Now get the hell outa here and get back to the Psyche. I'll let you know."

I figured that was about the story.

So here I was, only this time I wasn't going down and out. Brother, I was there. I'd had it, and the vultures were already circling around to pick at the pieces.

Right now, half the cops in L.A. were sleeping, and the other half had their holsters unflapped, looking for me.

The car came to the crest of a hill, the lights hit the low clouds, then settled back on the wet, twisting road. The rain beat down harder, and the car was buffeted even more by rising ocean winds. Far beneath, the surf roared and howled, trying to get up to the coastal road.

San Pedro was five miles away, and the rest of the trip would have to be made on my own two feet. I cut off the main highway and slowly drove and slid down a slippery, muddy lane. The trees above sheltered me a little, acting as rigid sentinels, because they knew me well from years back.

I turned to the right at the open spot where years before I had done a lot of talking to many interested girls. The place was a sort of arena, and when the moon used to rise over the hills, it didn't take much of an imagination to visualize Pan dancing around on his hind feet, blowing on his pipes and calling the other pagan gods to order.

But now there was no moon, and the rains started with a new, mad fury. To the west, more clouds were rolling landward, and I sat and watched them fight for position. I sat smoking a cigarette and trying to plan ahead. But my mind was a blank, a clean slate that had no answer for me, except eventual capture and death. I nodded in agreement with it and looked into the embers of the cigarette for some sane answer. But it merely got fainter and winked understandingly back. I tossed it from the window, and I envied it for its quick death in a muddy puddle of water.

I slid the car into low gear and rode along with it for fifty feet before I stepped out. It had occurred to me that it would be better for everyone all around if I stayed with the car. But I was a coward and stood in the driving rain while the car bumped its solitary way down the uneven slope. It went slowly, maybe even a little sadly.

Once it seemed to nod good-by. At any rate, I gave it a little salute, which it seemed to acknowledge as it hesitated, half turned around, then plunged over the sheer cliff to the rocks a hundred feet below. It made a roaring grind of rage and pain, then there was nothing but silence as the storm and wind took over the theme again, supported by the unhappy beating of my heart.

My car gone, my past was dead, and my future was a crepe-hung uncertainty. God, I could have used a drink!

My knees trembled and begged me to sink down and pray, but I had forgotten how. I'd been at the top, where a man forgets he needs God.

Well, God, I'm not praying, but just give me an even break. And let me get those dirty bastards who tried to frame me!

An hour and a half later, I reached the housing project northwest of San Pedro. I had been walking since time began, and my feet and legs were wet and aching. I turned inside, slopped through deep puddles without really caring, and stumbled toward an apartment that was awake. In the kitchen a man plodded back and forth, bending now and then to put coffee on the stove, or clean up last night's dishes. I figured his wife was probably in bed, wishing that he wouldn't make so much noise when he got ready to go to work.

I knocked at the door and waited, feeling like a tramp about to enter St. Patrick's Cathedral, seeking sanctuary. Footsteps beat across the bare floor, it opened, and a man stood looking at me.

"Car stalled out a mile or so north of here. Got to get to town and get a mechanic so's I can get to San Diego. Use your phone for a cab?"

"Sure, c'mon in. God, you're soakin'. Have a cuppa coffee while you're waitin'. Take off your coat and sling it over the chair by the oven."

My nerves were a string of firecrackers, and if anyone had poked me, I'd have gone off into popping hysterics. Mine host was a swell guy and gave me a stack of toast and a slug of marmalade while we waited for the cab. I finished eating, chewing on my nerves for dessert till the cab blasted its horn out in the darkness.

"Thanks a lot, pal."

He shrugged it off. "Forget it. Hope you can get a mechanic this early. Luck!"

"I'll need it."

The sleepy cab driver managed to stay awake long enough to drive me to an all-night grocery store. I was stunned when I discovered that I had only a couple of twenties. I spent over half of it on groceries, solid things like beans, corn, canned meats, and two cartons of cigarettes. Some wine went well with the purchases, also, but I had to buy that under the counter, because it wasn't six o'clock yet.

I carried the boxes to the cab, dumped them inside, and told the yawning driver to take me down Twenty-second Street to the boat landing.

For the last few feet to the boat, I did nothing but sweat my life away, thinking that the cops might be there, waiting in the darkened cabin, guns drawn, scowling, waiting for me. I picked my cautious way over the shiny, slippery deck, placed the box on top of the cabin, and opened the door.

My breath was a happy thing as it gushed out when the vacant cabin stared up at me welcomingly. The driver helped me with my packages. I gave him five dollars for his troubles, and he left yawning.

Time was the most precious thing in the world as I started the engine. It coughed protestingly, died, started again beneath my demanding hand, grunted once, and caught hold. While it warmed up, my nervous eyes jerked toward the storm-warning flags that were stiffened out in the rushing wind.

My head shook and called itself a fool to be attached to the likes of me. A cabin cruiser had no right to be out in the storm and towering waves. But my mind spoke up like an obedient servant and said it had to be that, or nothing.

I backed the boat away from the slip, looked over my shoulder, and saw its steady exhaust steaming up through the little ripples. The boat ground into gear and curved away from the land, and life as I had known it. I pointed the nose toward the harbor opening, and even before I reached it, the waves started pummeling the ship. She seemed to resent it, because she fought back valiantly and met each one squarely.

A ghostly tanker, barely visible through the gray dawn, was riding low and full in the heavy swells, making its slow way seaward from Long Beach Harbor. Its radar antenna was methodically scanning the murk of fog and rain, and probably picked me up as a futile blob off its starboard side. I envied every man on board for his safety and freedom, and would have given my chance for heaven to be there instead of here, letting any of them change places with me.

If you've ever run away, you understand the feeling and know what a desolate, all-gone sensation it is. You feel like crying all over the place and tucking your tail in between your legs.

Or jumping overboard to meet oblivion squarely.

Or getting roaring drunk.

Drunk! The idea of the day!

I reached inside the locker, one hand on the wheel and two eyes on the grayness of the sea, and brought out a nearly full bottle of Old Grand-Dad. I was happy to see the old man and felt like chucking him under the chin just to see him giggle. A drink was never more welcome, and as it fanned out in my ready stomach, I blessed whoever it was who thought up whisky.

The driving rain started again and slanted down against the windshield. The cabin had started to warm up. I lit a cigarette and inhaled, felt the warmth invade my lungs, and grinned. Once again life was improving. *Improving!* Ha, that made a lot of sense. It couldn't have got any worse. The boat rocked back and forth uncertainly, and I braced myself to keep my brains from being spilled out all over the cabin.

I put the Treble Clef—what a name to tack on a boat!—on a magnetic heading of 103 degrees after I lost sight of the land and followed the compass down toward Dana Point. The coastline was a dead, forgotten thing as we plunged along. Now and then the boat would show her skirts to the water, and the propeller would futilely bite at the air. But on the whole she did herself proud and fought back when she had to.

The low ceiling lifted about noon, the storm slid overhead, and the coastline and green hills came alive. I blessed God for dividing the water from the land, then started checking landmarks. The waves smoothed out. The boat and I were grateful and skimmed along over the water. At two o'clock I swung hard aport toward land. As I put into an isolated cove, the blue sky was peeking through, accented by the receding clouds. I steered carefully in through the rocks and switched off the engine.

The cove was like a beer bottle, wide at the bottom and narrow at the entrance where the foamy waves broke in. More than once I had used it, but always for fun, never life. I sighed and poured a sane drink in an ounce jigger. I threw it into my mouth and sat down on the seat to think.

I was at least three miles from the Dana Point yacht landing, where the bigger boats moored. It was a good bet that none of them were as small as mine, and the owners would be cautious people who wouldn't go out in the sea for a few days. So I was safe, I hoped.

I fished out paint and other things and went to work. By nightfall, the Treble Clef had been replaced by the Sea Wind, a good virile name, and I had scrambled the last four license numbers from 5728 to 8725 just in case the Coast Guard happened to glance at me later on. When I shaved that evening, I left a mustache growing and squinted my eyes, trying to decide how I would look with one of those things.

From the clothes locker I pulled out my seagoing rags, placed my cap on at what I hoped was a rakish angle, and sat down to a meal of corned-beef hash, fried beans, fruit salad, and coffee. The old man on the bottle watched me eat, then seemed to smile broadly as I uncorked him and poured a healthy slug into the black coffee. I hummed a little tune, relaxed on the bunk, and thought of Mardi.

Don't worry, baby, I haven't forgotten you. But what the devil could I do? I had to run to live to return and conquer.

Conquer! Ha! I had as much chance of beating Manny and Grebel as I had of playing piano solo at Carnegie Hall. The waves slipped through the rocks into the cove and played gently on the sides of the boat. They had a friendly sound.

For the next five days I stayed in my own little heaven till I started talking to the Sea Wind. That wouldn't have been so bad—every man talks to his boat—but when she started answering me back, I knew the time had come for me to seek human companionship for a few hours. It just wouldn't be fair to give them a driveling idiot to wheel to the death house.

I unlatched the dinghy and rowed a half mile south till I found a steep path that led like a snarled ball of yarn up the side of the cliff. I tied the boat to some jutting rocks, and before night had completely taken over, I had dragged myself up to the top of the cliff, a couple of hundred feet above the ocean as the stone drops. I lay panting for long minutes, then pulled myself erect and headed down a crooked dirt road.

For at least fifteen minutes I walked toward the coast highway, trying to keep in the shadows of tall bushes and steering away from homes. I rounded the last curve and saw a blinking neon sign on the highway.

"Beer—Beer."

I started running. My panting lungs and aching legs demanded that I rest before entering the oasis. I leaned behind the café on the south side and gradually sobbed my way back to normal breathing. Then I slicked my hair back, felt for my money, and puckered my lips up into a gay whistle. I strode around in front as if I owned the world and an iron-clad option on Mars.

I walked inside and found myself face to face with two California state policemen.

CHAPTER EIGHT

M Y HEART begged to die, and I had to plead with it to keep pumping. To run out when both of them turned their heads to look at me would have been nothing less than self-murder. I looked away from them and sat down on a stool a few feet from theirs. While I waited for the waitress, I looked over my shoulder and saw their black-and-white sedan parked in the shadows on the north side of the café, out of sight of the entrance.

A red-haired waitress with a body that couldn't be hidden even behind her uniform came tripping up. We looked at each other, and it was like seeing someone I had known for years. Her dark-green eyes started working on me. Her smile was friendly and showed the whitest teeth I had ever seen. She had a well-scrubbed, clean look about her that I liked. Her lips were nice and crushable with no more than a trace of lipstick, and when she put her hands on the counter, they were clean, and the fingers were long and pretty.

We stopped looking at each other, and she said, "Yes, sir. May I help you?"

If my glands hadn't been atrophied in the last two minutes, my thoughts might have been lecherous. She seemed to read something in my eyes, and smiled a little. She ran the pinkest tongue in captivity over her lips and waited for me to settle back to normal.

"Got any draft beer, miss?"

"No, sir, only bottled. Do you like Eastern or Western?"

My laugh was pitiful, like the squeak of a trapped mouse. "Make it Western. I haven't been paid off yet."

One of the cops turned away from his coffee. I could feel him study me and reach into his mental file of wanted criminals. I guess the mustache covered up for me, because his voice was casual and friendly.

"Work around here?" he asked.

I turned to him. His face was beefy, but nice, and while his eyes were sharply alert, they weren't icy. His partner might have been cut from the same cloth. Their eyes weren't cop's eyes; they belonged to a couple of working men who were talking to another one.

"Yeah, more or less. I'm on James H. Knightly's Voltaire. We're moored at the landing. We're picking up supplies, then heading south again for the Galapagos. The old boy's got another yearning for treasure hunting. I guess when you've got half the money in the world you can afford to be eccentric." I shrugged and laughed.

"Yeah," one of them sighed. "I wouldn't know. Where were you during the storm?"

Yeah, where was I? Smack dab in the middle of it!

"We picked it up two days out of Acapulco. The tail end, that is. As it was, it was bad enough. What a way to make a living!"

"Try *our* job someday! When did you get in?"

"Couple of hours ago. I had a phone call to make, so he let me off. I'm first mate and chief deckhand; I shoulda stayed around and tucked him in bed. It's a nice enough setup. There's no kick comin'."

I shrugged again, but they didn't know that I was trying to shake off the screaming meemies. The girl walked up again.

"All we have in Western is Acme. Is that O.K.?"

"Sure, I like it. I don't think they have a singing commercial, do they?"

One of the cops laughed. "Hey, Kenny, didja see that damned-fool commercial on television? They had this box of matches..." Their voices retreated, and I began to relax a little and fished for my money. The girl returned with the beer, and never had one looked so good before. She poured it neatly into the glass.

I coughed a couple of times, and the tight band across my chest seemed to get looser. The first beer died almost as if I had inhaled it, and I nodded for another one. She brought it back with my change.

"Here you are, fifty cents out of ten dollars, and here's some change for that phone call." She placed the money in my hand, and when hers left, the long fingers seemed to glide along my palm, reluctant to leave.

The policemen were finishing their coffee just as their radio squawked out in the darkness. "C'mon, Bob, let's mosey along," the first one said. He slapped a coin down on the counter and started past me, then stopped and laid his hand on my shoulder. I almost died, I swear it, and my heart leaped upward, trying to get out and surrender. But the hand was friendly, and its grip was light.

"Good luck, buddy. Can't say as I envy you bein' out in that storm at night. So long, Doris!" he called.

" 'By, fellows!" she answered. "Thanks!"

The door slammed behind them, and I barely made it to the rest room before I threw up. In great crying sobs, I lost everything, including the beer. When I stopped, I wiped my mouth and tried to grin at myself in the mirror. But it was weak, and my eyes looked at me pityingly.

"You poor damned fool!" they said accusingly. "You'll never make it if you're going to do that every time you see a cop. Brace up, be a man, or we'll leave you! Now get out of here, go talk with that girl and get some strength in your backbone!"

I nodded, promised them I would, and went back to the counter. The girl was standing as if she had been waiting for me to return. She was pretty, red hair and all, and something told me that it was the real color, because her complexion was fair and soft, the kind that goes with auburn hair. When I sat down and looked into her eyes, I saw that they weren't really dark; it had been a trick of lighting. They were green with tiny brown flecks.

She stood erect and stretched a little.

"How's the beer?" she asked.

"Fine. Do you suppose you could make me a hamburger? I'm starved, for some reason."

She nodded as if she were really glad to do something for me, then she started another one without asking me when she saw how the first one was fading away. I noticed that she left the onions out of the second one. I started to joke about it, then for some reason changed my mind.

For the next two hours, we talked and laughed, getting more friendly with each joke. I bought her a beer, then she bought me one, and we got to know each other by our first names—Doris and Jack. Once when she arose, her hair brushed against my face, and it smelled clean and good. Who the devil wants perfume on hair, anyway?

"What about your phone call, Jack? I might kidnap you before the evening's over. Are you calling your wife?" she asked, and I noticed that she didn't let her breath out till I said:

"I'm not married. No woman would be nuts enough to have me."

"Oh, I don't know. I've seen lots worse."

"Sure, but not without a keeper on one end of their chain."

Her laughter was low and rippling like water in a clear stream. She was in a friendly mood, and all I had to do was grin now and then; she kept the conversation moving along. A few times we were interrupted by short orders, but she had staked her claim on me and shoveled the burgers and fries out in a big hurry.

Several times she mentioned my call, and something inside seemed to be hammering at me to make one. But to whom?

Certainly not Mardi; it was an odds-on chance that her lines would be tapped. Or Manny, because when I went calling on him, it would be with a .45, along with a loaded bazooka strapped over my shoulder. But God, it would be nice to talk with someone who ...

Cecil! Sure, why not? The guy was probably square; most gay people are, and God knew that I would be needing a friend. The future was lining itself up in front of me, straight, like a road with no turning or side streets. Far away at the end, just this side of the horizon, was the future meeting with the Gold Dust Twins, Manny and Grebel. And just beyond that on the time track were two freshly dug graves with a solitary figure leaning over them. From this distance in time, I couldn't make out who it was.

I turned back to Doris. "Got an L.A. directory?"

"Sure, under the counter." She leaned forward in her seat and reached over the counter, fished around, and brought out a beat-up jacketless version of a directory. The A's and B's were gone, and at the back, everything stopped at the Y's. But the Would You? Café was there, and I mumbled the number to myself as I went to the pay phone on the wall.

I recognized Cecil's voice as soon as he answered.

"Would You?" he said.

I grinned. "I might've, Cecil, but you should've asked me last week."

He drew in his breath, then gasped out, "Jackie?"

"None other, my friend."

"You're not in town, are you?" His voice was worried.

"Not quite, but I may be there soon, and I'm going to be needing a friend. Do you know where I can pick one up?"

"Look no further, doll. What can I do?"

"Nothing now. A lot later on, maybe. Have the cops been in there looking for me?"

"The only coppers who come in here are the regular Vice Squad boys, trying to cadge a free drink. No one's asked about you."

I grunted, trying to think, wishing that Mardi were near me. Her presence would restore everything to its normal position of sanity. When Cecil spoke again, it was a low, hissing sound, and I could imagine his eyes eagerly alert, working for a choice piece of news.

"Jackie, I'd like to ask a question."

"I know what it is, Cecil. No, I didn't kill him!"

"Shoot!" he cried. "And I was hoping you had. I own a piece of this bar, and I had to pay him eighty-five a week just to stay open."

"What do the papers say?"

"About the same thing as the wild winds. They all know you did it, except maybe the Daily Window, that tabloid. They're getting a large charge out of the whole mess. Flossie Narbonne is writing your life story side by side with Moss's."

"That's interesting. Say, Cecil, got a phone at your house?"

"I should say so. Western six-nine-six-nine. And it isn't a house, it's a cozy little apartment."

"I'll *bet* it is. Do you have a car?"

"No, but I can always borrow one from one of the tramps who come in here."

"Bless you, Cecil. One of these days I'll be seeing you. And don't forget, my grubby little life is in your little pink hands. For God's sake, don't tell anyone you talked with me."

"I won't. You can depend on me."

"Have you seen my—friend?"

"Oh, the girl? No, she hasn't been in here since the night you left with her. She called twice, asking about you."

I thought a second. "O.K., if she calls again, you *still* haven't seen me. 'By, Cecil."

" 'By, Jackie," he murmured.

When I returned, a fresh beer was sitting proudly next to my empty glass. By the time I had the gurgling beer poured, Doris came up front. She wore fresh lipstick and an aura of subtle, friendly perfume.

"I've got a quarter, Jack. What would you like to hear?"

"Your heart beating. Does that cost a quarter?"

She laughed delightedly; that was the first verbal pass I had made. "It might cost a lot more—or nothing. Depending."

My interested eyes followed her as she bent down to study the song titles. The skirt got familiar with her slender hips and rode upward on her pretty legs. She poked five buttons and returned. My eyes got all tangled up in her pert breasts.

The juke box clicked and hummed, the record scraped till the music started. And then guess what the first number was. Jack Griffith singing "Tonight We Love."

She sat down next to me, put an arm on my shoulder, then drew it back as if she had burned it. I couldn't help jumping myself; it was as if she had placed a red-hot poker on me. Her eyes got hazy, and her lips were suddenly soft and red.

"I played that song for you, Jack."

"Thanks. How come?" My throat was cotton dry, and the fast gulp of beer didn't really help it. I was afraid to hear her reply.

"Because I like you." She leaned forward, her eyes begging me to believe that they didn't belong to a cheap woman. "I thought..." and she stopped, running a nervous tongue over her lips.

"Thought what?" I asked, and my heart started thumping against my ribs. I knew damned well what she thought, but if things were going to seem right, she had to tell me.

"I thought that maybe we could go to my place for a drink. I close here in half an hour."

Because I was lonely and liked her, but more truthfully because I needed love and a woman's arms, I nodded. "If you'd like to, I guess I could use a drink. Do you live in town?"

"Just this side, half a block off the highway." She grinned, more at ease. "If you get frightened, you can run away."

"That's swell, but what'll you do if *you* get scared?"

"Maybe I don't scare easily."

Our eyes looked at each other with a glance as old as the first two people. Then she averted hers, thought a minute, and laughed. She reached over the counter and started fishing again. Within a couple of seconds she had found her purse, one of those overnight affairs, reached inside it, and brought out the prize catch of the season: a half pint of bonded whisky.

"Sometimes I get cold on the way home."

I rubbed my hands together. "Yeah. Me, too. Join me in a drink, podner—with your whisky?"

"Sho 'nuff!" We both laughed, then suddenly her lips were very close, waiting for mine to make the first move. My mouth swooped down, our lips met and clung tightly together. Her green eyes closed. She sighed. My hands wanted to start roaming, but I kept them under control, then slowly, reluctantly, took my mouth away.

Half an hour later, we climbed from her '40 Packard and walked inside. Her small home sat back from the street in a large lot, and backed onto an alley, fifty feet or so from the coast highway. The place was neatly proud of itself, and yet had the comfortable air of looking lived in. The living room ran the entire width of the house, and was cozy, containing a divan, a couple of easy chairs, and a writing desk. On the coffee table were a couple of magazines and an ash tray with a solitary lipstick-branded cigarette stub.

She told me where to dig out more whisky and disappeared. I took my time building two drinks, had a straight shot on the side, and started looking for her. The light was off in the living room, and I turned toward the bedroom. The door was open. I rapped lightly and walked in, holding the two drinks in the big paw I call my left hand.

She was lying in bed, in a frothy, lacy thing she probably called a nightgown, idly thumbing through a magazine that she couldn't possibly have been reading. An uncertain smile got braver as it flitted across her lips.

I handed her the two drinks.

It's hard to explain why, but it was as natural and healthy as marriage. When I slid into the bed she handed me back my drink. We finished them. She reached up behind her and switched off the bed lamp. I got one glimpse of a smooth, high breast, then there was nothing but soft darkness—and her.

She was at once warm and vibrant, alive and demanding in my arms. Her body was sweet as it took my love and responded to my questioning hands. Her kisses were warm and moist as her mouth joined mine. She sighed and she whispered, "Be good to me. It's been a very long time," and then there were no more words, because my mouth covered her lips, her arms went about me.

Long minutes later, her fingers tightened, then she fell away, her mouth open, her eyes closed. At last she kissed me gratefully on the mouth, and I put my arms more tightly around her.

After a while, when we were lying quietly, she spoke.

"Jack..."

"Hmm?"

"Who are you? Really, I mean."

"A sailor."

"Good night, Jack."

"Yeah. Good night."

The next morning, I awakened early before the gray dawn had given way to the brilliant sun. Her relaxed face was something from the pages of a study in beauty, and her lips were parted in a smile. If she was dreaming, she must have been enjoying it, and for a jealous moment I wished that I could peek inside her sleep and see it also.

In the bathroom I found a razor and started to shave. As the happy blade glided back and forth over my stubble, I started humming. Then, without realizing it, I commenced singing the song of the night before, "Tonight We Love."

There was a knock at the door.

"Breakfast's ready—Mr. Griffith!"

CHAPTER NINE

THE SONG DIED, rattling in my throat, and as I stood there, goose pimples blossomed on my arms and legs. My heart said, "So long, Boss!" and tried to jump out. In the next half minute, I cut myself twice, then rinsed the blood off and stepped into the kitchen. Doris was standing, waiting for me. She got on her tiptoes, demure, bridelike, eyes raised to mine and lips ready for a kiss.

There was a newspaper in her hand. Her look was meant to be childlike and innocent, but her twinkling eyes gave her away. I walked to her slowly, and without speaking took the paper from her hands.

There were two pictures of me on the third page, one the sexed-up glamour shot that had dragged 'em in at the Psyche. The other was a real-life snapshot of me in my sailing rags. I hadn't had a mustache when a friend took the picture the summer before, but she had thoughtfully penciled it in, and there I was, a dead ringer for a dead goose. I looked at her, and as she read my face, her eyes changed from mirth to pity. She took the paper from my trembling hand and put it on the table. Her arms went about me.

I held her back at arm's length. "Did you know about me last night?"

She shook her head. "Not till this morning. While you were shaving, I went out and got the paper, saw the pictures, then checked the back issues and knew that it was you. I don't know whether I'm happy or sad, but I think I liked my sailor better."

"Bless you, Doris. I love you for that."

She led me to the table and pushed me down, then dished up bacon and scrambled eggs and slid in next to me. While she started eating, I read the paper avidly, then nearly fainted when I came to the third paragraph.

I had been identified as the man who purchased the gun that had killed Moss.

This was the frame-up of all time!

It had been bought at a Third Street pawnshop, and experts had compared my handwriting with the signature on the shop's records. They were certain that I had signed the papers.

If I'd had that gun right then, I swear I'd have blown my brains out.

There wasn't a word about Manny. Only me. The murderer.

Or about Mardi, and I worried more about her than I did my own future.

Doris was silent and ate without saying a word. After breakfast she led me into the living room and gently pushed me into a chair. She cleaned up the dishes, then returned with steaming coffee. I was standing by the curtains, working overtime on my poor beat-up fingernails. As far as the papers were concerned, I was already in the gas chamber, waiting for the chemical reaction that would turn my future into a very dim thing.

"Coffee, Jack," she said. "I'll join you, then we can do some thinking."

We sat down on the divan together, and after a long kiss, she spoke. "Did you really kill him, or isn't it any of my business?"

"You know it is. You can't be here with a man, afraid that he'll ax-murder you sometime during the next minute. No, I didn't do it. But I know who did, and when I tried to tell the cops, they wouldn't listen worth two beats on the drums. That's why I took off at high port. It was the only way."

And then I told her the whole story, and when I was through, her eyes were sad for me. "How are you going to clear yourself, Jack?"

"You tell me. It's worth a lot to know. I don't have any idea."

Her hand squeezed mine. "You can stay here as long as you want to."

I looked into her green eyes, and loved them for their lack of coyness.

"Thanks, Doris, but I can't stay. Those cops saw me last night. Eventually they're going to remember something, and I'm allergic to getting my best friend in a jam with the law. I'm shoving off."

"How did you get here?"

"In my boat. It's anchored in a cove beneath the cliff, just north of the place where you work."

Her eyes were startled. "Then you *can't* go! I heard them talking last night about searching the coast from San Diego to San Luis Obispo. If they found your boat, you wouldn't stand a chance. Jack!" And then suddenly she jumped from the divan and stood trembling.

A car had stopped in front. I got up and peeked from behind the curtains. The black-and-white police car of last night had stopped, and the same two men got out and walked toward the house. The two red lights on the front of the car reminded me of sudden, bloody death. Doris looked over my shoulder, and we were the world's two best candidates for blood transfusions.

Without saying a word, she grabbed me by the hand, rushed me into the bedroom, and pointed at a closet. I hated myself for a coward as I hid behind the dresses that smelled perfumed and friendly. Doris' slippers clicked into the living room, rushed about, then ran into the kitchen. She turned on the water tap and started clinking dishes together. She sang in a sweet, clear voice, and the rattling dishes joined in the chorus and carried the theme well. A demanding hand beat against the front door. She stopped her singing, and I could imagine her grabbing a towel to wipe her hands as she walked to the door.

"Yes?" she called gaily. "Who is it?"

"State police, Kenny and Bob. May we come in, Doris?"

"Why, sure. Just a moment." The safety chain rattled, the lock relaxed, and two men tromped in. Her voice was surprised. "Still on duty? You boys look tired. What's the matter?"

"Do you remember that fellow who came into the café last night?"

"Which one? There were so many. Oh, you mean the Joe who came in while you were having your coffee?"

"That's right. This one." I could imagine the picture coming from his pocket, and almost was able to see the stage frown disappear from Doris' face when she recognized it.

"Yes, he's the one. What did he do?"

"He's wanted in L.A. on a murder charge. Do you know anything about his actions after we left?"

"I—don't remember too well, but I think he left after an hour or two. No, wait a minute. He stayed longer than that. About eight o'clock a woman came in, and they left right after that."

"Which direction?"

"South, toward San Diego. Oh!" she squealed. "A murderer!"

"Seems like that," the other man said. His voice got cute. "Reckon we oughta search the place, Kenny?"

I almost lost my breakfast, and my bent knees were a couple of cold, soft-boiled eggs. Then I thought of the two coffee cups and the paper that had been folded up in the direction of the picture on which she had drawn a mustache, and prayed for immediate death.

"Might be a good idea, at that, Bob. This cute li'l thing never gives us a tumble, so she must have somebody on the side."

"You fellows!" she laughed. "I'm still faithful to you. I love you both because you pay for your coffee, even though you *do* chase away all of my convict trade. How about a cup of coffee now, on the house for a change?"

The first voice got "cop" in it again. "No, thanks, Doris. We'd better be moving along. As it is, we're in hot water for not recognizing him last night." His voice got louder as his footsteps came into the bedroom, stopping within three feet of where I crouched, sweating my life's blood away. He walked back into the front room. "Thanks anyway, honey. We'll see you this evening."

"Well, for heaven's sake! What else do you know about him? That's just like a man, leaving a woman all up in the air!"

Kenny roared, "I'd never leave *you* up in the air!" All three of them laughed. "There's nothing much to tell. They found a dinghy tied up this morning at the foot of the big hill, and located his cruiser a little ways north. That's how we got wise to him. We were going to come earlier, but we didn't want to disturb your beauty nap. We've been working all night."

"I'm sorry," she said. Then Bob said something I didn't catch, and the three of them started laughing together. I could imagine her white teeth shining impartially from one to the other, and for some reason I felt jealous.

"Well, let's radio the Sheriff, Bob. S'long, Doris."

"Take it easy, fellows, and get some sleep. I'll see you tonight."

The door opened and shut, the safety chain rattled again, and the feet marched away. I slumped to the floor. The hem of one of her frilly dresses tickled my nose; I brushed it away just as the closet door opened and she grinned down at me. I stared up at her through two gauzy things and tried to smile. But it was weak, and I wouldn't have given a dime for it on the open market.

Her eyes were gleeful, and her nose crinkled up. "All right, lover boy, get off it and pay me for my lies! God's gonna write down a lot of black marks for me today."

I tried a grin on for size. It didn't fit very well, so I said weakly, "The cups and paper—what'd you do with them?"

"I'm a neat housekeeper. I picked the paper up and tossed it on top of the burned bacon. You wasteful thing!" she grinned accusingly. "I washed the coffee cups like any good housewife."

I struggled to my feet, rubbed my aching legs, and kissed her. She put her arms around me, then we collapsed on the bed, laughing like two darned fools.

God, it was good to be alive!

For the next four days I played housewife behind the drawn curtains, never going outside, kept the place tidied up, and barked my shins on the furniture at night in the pitch-dark rooms. During the days, several people knocked on the door, but it was always the typical salesman's rapping, so I didn't worry too much.

The papers and Doris, through Kenny and Bob, kept me posted on Operation Manhunt. I had been seen south of the border down Tijuana way, in Calexico, Palm Springs, and Los Angeles. Once an eager starlet's press agent talked her into saying that she had picked me up in Santa Monica. "I always like to help people out," she told the reporters, "so naturally when I saw this poor man trudging along, I stopped and offered him a ride. He started getting fresh, so I stopped and pointed to the curb. 'Get out and walk!' I said. He turned and went into a bar." I cursed her out and prayed that the studio would drop her option. God! How low can you reach for publicity?

That fourth night, Doris seemed to sense something when she walked in around eleven-fifteen. She had been smiling when she entered, and for the first time I didn't rise and greet her with a kiss. She saw my face and walked slowly toward me. Her coat started dragging on the floor. She dropped it and slumped on the floor by the divan. Her lips were inches from mine.

"What gives, sailor?"

The smile on my face was weaker than a day-old kitten, and I tried to make up for it with a meaningless gesture. "Gotta be leaving, honey."

She nodded. "It was too much fun to last, wasn't it?"

"Much too much!" I leaned over and kissed her mouth. For a long time it belonged to me, then I drew away. "I hate to go, but that's the way things stand. I'm getting fat and lazy."

Tears welled up in her eyes, and she was impatient with herself for having shown them. She jerked her head, trying to throw them off, and said, "Take me with you! I won't get in the way, and maybe I can help."

My head shook sadly, meaning it. "You know I can't do that. Things are going to go from bad to worse, and I don't want you getting hurt."

She hid her face and started sobbing. My mouth drooped open like an idiot, and for the first time I felt clean and humble inside. Her shaking increased; her body tensed and pressed against mine, seeking comfort. I arose slowly, gathered her into my arms, and carried her into the bedroom.

For a long time I held her close to me, touching and caressing her gently. Then the crying wore itself out, and her mouth sought mine blindly, wildly. Then she lay back and looked up at the ceiling.

"I'm sorry," she said quietly. "It won't happen again. I've never been in love before, and I don't think I like the feeling; it hurts too much. I was married once. We lived together for only three months, and he was the first man I had ever been with. You were the second. I don't know why I did it, but I was suddenly lonesome, and I wanted you.

"I thought at first I was a nasty woman, but I didn't care. Then you showed me real love for the first time in my life. And now, even though I'm going to lose you, I don't care. I'm glad."

"I love you for that, Doris."

"But you don't love me!"

What could I honestly tell her?

I leaned over to kiss her.

"Maybe I do, and maybe I don't, Doris. I can't be sure. There are too many things on my mind to think about love. My life is hanging by a thread that's getting weaker every day. Maybe after it's all over ..."

"No, that's just what I *don't* want!" she cried vehemently. "After it's all over, I wouldn't be the same person you left, and you would have changed, too. I couldn't stand to have you nice to me just because you felt sorry."

"Doris, there's no part for you in what's going to happen next! Can't you understand?"

She sat up and leaned over me. "All right, how long do you think you would last when a policeman saw you? I know you a little by this time and realize that you have a temper. The policeman would see you and try to arrest you, then you'd do something foolish and he'd kill you. Jack, you're too well known to go up there alone. They'd find you the minute you came to town."

"All right, baby, so they get me. Then I'll have lots of talking to do."

"*Talking!* After you ran away, do you think they'd believe you? And besides, if that Lieutenant Grebel is in crooked politics, he's probably not alone. You wouldn't stand a chance. That little Manny has got a perfect alibi by this time, and—Jack, darling, I swear I won't try to hang onto you, but you must have help! I'll die, I really mean it. Life won't be worth living if they kill you!"

I pulled her down next to me and kissed her wet eyes. I took her head in my arms and put it on my shoulder.

"What's your idea, Doris?"

She was instantly eager and squirmed up again. "I've thought it all out. I've been talking about quitting for a long time. Tonight I did. They won't suspect anything."

"I won't drag you into this mess!"

"*You won't!*" Her face was almost scornful. "I've been in it ever since the first night you came here. You changed everything, made things seem good and holy. I fell in love with you, Jack, so I'm already in anything you are."

I lay back on the bed for a long time, trying to get my thoughts in line. She was silent while I made my decision. Finally I said: "All right. We'll go together."

CHAPTER TEN

T HE NIGHT was bitingly cold, and inland the orange ranchers were firing up their stinking smudge pots, and the next day housewives and citizens would be cursing them out.

We loaded her bags into the car, and I slid behind the wheel and started toward Los Angeles and Manny and Grebel and Johnny Law, who would shoot me on sight. The stars were out, and here and there towering, snow-white clouds meandered through the sky, going nowhere in particular, and in no hurry to get there.

An hour before, the crescent moon had slid into the plunging sea, and the Pacific coast was getting ready to go to bed. Everyone except Doris and Jack, that is. I turned the heater on, the car warmed up, and she sat cuddled next to me, her head resting on my shoulder as she hummed a little tune.

Presently she lit two cigarettes, put one between my lips, and leaned back. "Where will we stay, Jack?"

"I've been thinking about that. We'd better settle for the South Gate area. They've got factories around there, and new arrivals won't be noticed. Now remember what I told you. We just got in from Pomona, and I'm going to get a job at the tire factory here. Does that story suit you?"

"Whatever you think, darling," she murmured.

I could have told her that according to my thoughts, she was number one in the Kiss Parade. Mardi seemed a vague dream at this moment. We drove up the twisting coast highway into Laguna and turned inland to the canyon that led through Santa Ana to Los Angeles.

"I hate to ask, Doris, but how much money do we have?"

"You have it. You should know."

"*I* should know. Honey, I haven't made any of that folding stuff since before you picked me up off your doorstep. Well, don't worry, I can borrow some from Cecil, a friend of mine."

"Jack, I put our money in your wallet."

I looked sideways at her. Her eyes turned toward mine and were round and innocent. I stopped the car, leaned over and kissed her, studied her pert face and huge eyes, then shook my head.

"For crying out loud, why?"

"Because you're the man in the family, as long as it *is* a family, and no man likes to have his wi—*girl* dole out the money."

I suddenly felt humble. "How did I ever rate you?"

She tossed her head, and the long curls flew out, brushing my face. "You just caught me at the right time, or I'd never have given you a second look."

"I'd have rippled my muscles at you!"

"*Muscles!*" she laughed. "Lover boy, I've seen you without that padded T shirt."

I grinned. "Doris, I…" I swear, I don't know what I was going to say, but my heart was full.

"Yes?" she asked eagerly.

"Nothing," I said flatly.

Atlantic Boulevard was a broad highway that existed merely for the beer parlors, filling stations, supermarkets, used-car lots, fortunetellers, stop signals, and other pests. The old street that had known me for years didn't bother to welcome me back; in fact, it didn't even know that I had been gone.

At Manchester Boulevard I swung into a drive-in for some chow. I bought a paper at the honor-system stand while the carhop made her date with a slick-haired pimp in a new Ford convertible.

After we ate, I fished for my wallet and opened the bulging thing. My eyes popped when I looked inside and riffled through the money. There was nothing smaller than a twenty, and there must have been at least fifty of them.

"Where the devil did you get the money, Doris?"

"It took a long time to save it up, Jack."

"And you trust *me* with it?"

She leaned against me and brushed my cheeks with her lips. "Of course. If you ever let me down, life wouldn't be worth living anyhow. You've got everything I own now, including my little heart."

My arm went about her. "I'll never let you down!"

"Darling, I'm not trying to buy you. I promise that later, when you don't need me, I'll disappear."

"You sound as if I'm going to win this little game."

Her eyes narrowed. "If you don't, *I'll* take over, and I'll make the Korean war look like a mountain feud."

Several people in the car next to us ogled over, making it time to leave. I blinked the car lights and waited for the check.

"I'll try to pay you back someday, Doris."

"You've already paid me back, just by making me live."

That night we slept in a motel in South Gate.

The next day I rented a small, walk-up-three-flights hole that the owners had the guts to call a penthouse apartment. But it was in South Gate, where I wanted to settle, just off Tweedy Boulevard, close to a super-duper market, and better yet, next door to a liquor store.

While Doris stocked up on groceries and such uninteresting stuff, I had the gas and lights turned on and went to the liquor store, where I bought a case of canned beer, several bottles of "cookin' whisky," some soda, and a sack of canned do-hickies for midnight snacks. I carefully got a receipt for the whole mess so I could pay Doris back in full someday. Ha! Laugh just as if you made a big joke, boy. If she ever wants to collect, she'll have to take up medium study and send you bills from this side of your lonely grave.

We spent the afternoon and early evening getting rid of the dirt the last tenants had left so ours could get a fresh start. Then I built two strong highballs, brought the liquor and mix into the living room, made another trip and came back with cashew nuts and ice cubes, then flopped on the divan. I lit our cigarettes and handed her a drink.

"Toast, baby?"

"What toast?" she asked fearfully.

"A toast to tomorrow, and all that goes with it."

"You mean that tomorrow you're ..."

"Yep, starting out. I've got to shovel a couple of devils down into hell."

Her mouth was suddenly tight, and her teeth bit down hard to keep from chattering. "Have you made any plans?"

"Just one. I'm going up to see Cecil, that friend I told you about. After that everything's a blank."

"Can you trust him?"

"I think so. At least, I've got to start somewhere, and I need a friend up there."

I explained to her just how Cecil fitted into the deadly jigsaw puzzle, then took a long drink to moisten my dry mouth. I remembered that I had never told Doris about Mardi and me. Always I had mentioned her as Moss's wife, never as the woman I wanted. Doris seemed to sense something; she looked at me closely, and I would have bet my soul against twenty Indian rupees that she was going to say what she did:

"Jack, are you in love with this Mardi?"

I tried to answer her casually, to laugh and shrug it off. I tried to bring my mouth under control to smother a lie. I wanted to tell her the truth, that I wanted Mardi more than my next breath, but I couldn't. So I said, "No."

"Yes, you are, Jack," she said quietly, and two great tears welled up from her soul and spilled over.

She broke down, sobbing. I kissed her tear-stained cheeks gently, and their taste was good.

"I'm sorry, Doris. More than you can ever know."

"I'm not, Jack, and I promise it won't happen again." She held me tighter, and her mouth was nearly touching mine as she spoke. "I'll never try to hold you," she promised. "Now, let's have another drink. For some silly reason, I'm thirsty."

CHAPTER ELEVEN

"WHO'S SMART in this town, Cecil?"

"Everybody's smart up here, Jackie."

"I need someone who's just a little smarter than everybody, but honest."

He frowned and shook his head. He wasn't dressed the way he had been at the Would You? He wore a pair of old slacks and a gray sport shirt. "You're asking for a lot. You don't get smart by being honest. In Hollywood, you get that way by selling secrets. To buy something, you sell something else. If you're smart, the thing you buy is better than what you sell, and costs less." He paused.

We were in his second-story apartment on Kenmore. A faint incense hung in the closed draperies, and the lights were low.

"Do you like my place?" Cecil asked.

I smiled and picked up my drink. "On you it looks good. If I wore it I'd feel queer."

"Queer!" he said in a low, bitter voice. "Don't get me started on that subject!"

I hid my face in the Martini glass. "Sorry, I didn't mean you, Cecil. Somehow I don't think of you that way."

He put his hand on my knee, but it was only a friendly gesture. "I know, Jackie. You're one of the few men I've ever known who doesn't look down on me. That's why I want to help you. Now let's get organized. Did you know that there's an underground reward out for you?"

My chest grew tight, and my knees were riddled with icicles. I sighed, but it was like the last breath in my lungs. "Alive, or … ?"

"You're smarter than that. Lots, but *lots* of people would like to see you dead so they could—"

"—drag my corpse by the scruff of the neck and toss the pelt on Manny's desk. I get it. Brother, *how* I get it."

Cecil stood looking down on me, his face a little sad.

"How much am I worth?" I asked.

"Alive, nothing. Dead, twenty thousand dollars."

"For what I know, the deal's cheap. Maybe I could work out something with him. Twenty grand for me if I leave the country and never return. What's the word on Manny now?"

"The smart money says he's moved up a notch. He's number one on this coast, pro tem. They're giving him a tryout for the permanent role. If he makes good, he's really in. If not—" Cecil shrugged.

"Who's the really big boss out West?"

"Victor Lamson. Noble-sounding name, isn't it? He holes out in Las Vegas most of the time. I've never seen him, but they say he has ulcers, a chronic heart condition, and a deadly fear of dying."

"Yeah, any fear of dying *would* be deadly. I know just how he feels. What about this Flossie Narbonne, who's been writing my story in the paper? Is she straight?"

"I think so. I know her a little, and she hates the whole crowd of hoodlums and thugs."

"Get her for me!"

"What?" he cried. "You'll be sticking your neck out."

"I've got to trust someone. How about you? You've got my neck in a vise, and if you wanted to turn the handle..." I made a crunching sound, and he paled a little, then felt his own neck and gulped.

"I'd never do that!"

"Sure, and I appreciate it, but I've got to have more help. Slip her the word—quietly, that is—and tell her I want to give her an exclusive interview."

"But that's dangerous! Look, she may be all right, but twenty thousand dollars has turned lots of honest heads in the wrong direction. On top of that, all sorts of people keep their eyes on her, where she goes and who she sees. It'll be hard!"

"All good things are hard, buddy. Will you do it?"

"All right, but don't blame me if things go wrong."

"I won't blame you. If they *do* go wrong, I won't be around to blame anyone."

I shuddered, realizing that it wasn't very funny, or very far from the truth. I got up and stood in front of him, putting my hands on his shoulders. "Be careful, Cecil. For God's sake, watch your step."

"Listen, I've been handling the Vice Squad for years, and I know my stuff. Any time you deal with those dogs and come out on top at least half the time, you know the score. You stay here, and I'll bring her back with me, if I have to drag her in by her wig."

He left, and my hand shook a little as it pulled the drapes aside. Cecil cut diagonally across the street at a half trot toward a cab stand.

I went to the stack of Daily Windows he had lying on a kitchen chair, brought them into the front room, and started to read my story. Flossie's picture was at the head of each column. She wore a grim smile; her lips were tightly clamped together like a hostile bulldog's. But they weren't the main, compelling feature. Her eyes were set deep into a middle-aged face; they were strong, resembling diamond drills that bit right through the camera lens onto the paper and into my eyes.

She was a pretty good writer, and if she had done her own leg work, she was the world's best reporter. She had dug up things about my past that I thought only I knew.

I finished reading the installments, and my tired hand dropped the last paper on the carpet. Without realizing it, my eyes closed, and I slept ....

Footsteps sounded on the stairs. I shuddered, jerked myself erect, and looked wildly about the room for a weapon. Several wrought-iron things were leaning against each other next to the fireplace. I grabbed a poker and jumped behind the door.

It opened slowly, and I was a rat in the world's best trap as I waited. There were no voices, and the poker was alert in my poised hand. Then Cecil's nervously bobbing face peeked around at me.

The air flew from my lungs and I slumped against the wall, wilting like a two-bit corsage. The poker drooped and scraped the floor as I tried to grin. Without moving, I said, "How did you know where I was, Cecil?"

"The mirror on the wall."

I looked to the right, into the mirror—and the clear, agate eyes of Miss Flossie Narbonne, she of the bulletproof corset and bribeproof pen. "Caustic" and "convincing" were good words for her writing, and as I looked into her forceful face, I knew why. She wouldn't run from anything, death included. She stepped into the room, looked quizzically at the poker, and said, "Are you two going steady?"

I smiled and tossed it onto the divan. "Self-preservation, whatever that means. You know who I am, Miss Narbonne?"

"Just call me Flossie. Even Moss used to call me that when he tried to buy me a quieter typewriter," she said as she peeled off her gloves.

I looked at them and couldn't help wondering if they were made from the hide of some petty crook she had skinned. She flopped on the divan. Her eyes were watching me closely, trying to make up their minds about the defendant who stood before the jury box. I tried to look manly, gave it up as a bad job, and walked into the kitchen.

"Drink, Flossie? I don't think Cecil minds my playing host."

"Straight whisky, if my little friend has it." Cecil had gone into the bedroom, getting made up for work later in the evening. He called through the closed door to tell me where the whisky was.

From the kitchen I yelled back to Flossie, "I knew a man once who took his whisky neat. Guess who!"

"Moss Morrison," her voice rang out. "He's taking them straight these days, too—straight from an asbestos glass."

I walked and stood over her with a double shot glass in my hand.

"Health, Flossie!"

She held it in front of her; her eyes were cautious. "What did you want with me, Mr. Griffith? I'm not a singer."

"Call me Jack." I got my drink and returned, squatting in front of her, Arab-like. "No, you don't sing, but you write, and maybe you could use a good story. It might be worth something."

Her eyes were more curious than anything else. "Let's hear it."

"I didn't kill Moss!"

"I feel like leaving. I'm disappointed. Why didn't you? He needed killing."

"Yeah, he felt sort of bad, too. He liked me, and would rather have had me kill him than the egghead who did."

She was suddenly alert, her senses eager. "Who killed him?"

"Manny Lewis, of the Psyche Ballroom Lewises."

She whistled softly. "Manny Lewis, the scourge of Sunset Boulevard. Was he playing Robin Hood?"

I sank back on the floor and gulped half of the drink in a hurry. "He was just playing hood. Do you believe me?"

"It's so damned much like Manny that I have to."

She sipped thoughtfully at her drink, looked into its friendly surface, then threw the entire two ounces in her mouth. She swallowed and made a face, then looked at me. "You poor joker, you're *really* in the oven!"

"Flossie, I need someone who's in the know in this town."

"A lot of people say that I am, but maybe they're just being nice. But go ahead."

"I hear Manny's moved up a notch."

She grunted. "That's right, and his head can't take the altitude. It's swelled up like a pregnant pumpkin seed."

"What do you know about a Lieutenant Grebel in Vice?"

"A bastard if I ever saw one, Jack."

"He knows where the body's buried, or I miss my guess."

"I don't doubt it. Now, let's have the whole story from start to finish. And be honest! I can smell out a lie before you can think of it."

I rubbed my chin. Yeah, the story; I knew it by heart. One day I had been a reasonably happy Sunset jerk, and the next … The words started spilling out, faster and faster, stumbling over each other in their eagerness to be heard. Flossie listened silently to me and lit one cigarette after another, and seemed to be searching for great truths in their glowing embers. She was silent for several minutes after I polished off my tale of woe. I poured another drink.

Cecil re-entered the room, ready for work, and sat quietly next to Flossie.

She looked at me. "Jack, you're right in the middle of a nice, tight frame. You'd look good in a stained-glass window. Yes, on you it would be becoming."

"You believe me?"

She shrugged. "Sure, but where's my story? Anyone can write obits."

I started to protest, then kept still when Cecil shook his head warningly. She walked around the room, pausing now and then to study me. I felt like a pauper's cadaver on the dissecting table at General Hospital. I gulped the drink down, trying to ignore Cecil's disapproving stare. At last he got up and walked to Flossie just as she was measuring me for a shroud; I could see it in her eyes, and it was a damned eerie feeling.

"Dear," he said, "I want to help the boy. Don't you?"

"Blunt little creature, aren't you, Cecil?"

He straightened up. "Don't you believe him, Flossie?"

"Cecil, I believe him, or I'd have left here before I got that next drink you're going to offer me."

Cecil smiled happily and scuttled for the kitchen. She looked at me again. This time I was a vile bug beneath the microscope, trying to look blasé and nonchalant. But I gave it up as a bad job, arose, and stretched.

"Guess why I was framed, Flossie."

"Am I a fool that you have to tell me? They needed a fall guy, and you were the best one they could find. You were well known, God knows why, and had a certain amount of fame—among the lower classes," she said, smiling as she put her hand on my drinking arm.

Cecil entered with a full glass. "Thanks, lover," she said. She turned back to me. "Like I say, Jack, I know these things. What's going on in your alleged brain?"

"Just one thing, Flossie. If the syndicate got word that Manny really killed Moss, they'd take care of him."

She shook her finger at me. "Relax, Profile, it won't work. The first thing to remember is that even if they took care of Manny, as you so cutely put it, that wouldn't help you. Manny would just disappear, and you'd get blamed. And who's going to tell them? You? I'm laughing. You'd be in a concrete overcoat before you could say, 'Tag!'"

"Could *I* tell them? I'm all out of laughs now, so I'm crying a little. My bosses give me a lot of room to play in, and I love 'em for it, but they won't let me get in too deep, like going to the syndicate with a story like that. Since I got in my last scrape, they make me clear everything concerning the big-time boys with the city desk before I try to tackle it. It's not that they love me, they just figure I help boost the circulation, and they want me alive. Besides, there are laws to protect people, even Manny, from libel."

"Libel-schmibel!" I cried. "The little bastard is guilty as the devil. You know it, I know it, God knows it!" I grabbed her shoulders. "What the hell do you think I asked you to come here for? I need your help, and you've got the reputation of being a damned good fighter. I'll admit I'm scared, but I'm going to fight them. Alone, or with your help! I'm mad now, damned mad. Don't worry, you won't be left out. You'll be there for the kill!"

She started to speak, then I realized that she was just being kind. She knew that it would probably be *my* kill, not Manny's that she would be writing about.

I shook her again, not very gently. "Flossie, honey, I've got to do something big. I have to get Manny before he gets me. I trust you and Cecil, but sure as sin, someone's going to see me within the next day or so, and Manny and that bastard Grebel will know that I'm back in the city. Then—then …"

Her voice was soothing as she patted me. "I know, precious. I—well …"

Cecil and I were the original Greek chorus as we both breathed, "Yes?"

"I'll do it! It may be the last story I'll ever work on, but so help me, I love it. It's something big, like trying to break the bank at Monte Carlo!"

"That's right, and we've got to roll a natural!"

"All right, let's sit down and think this out." She rubbed her hands together, sat down, and kicked off her shoes. She massaged her feet absently. "Cecil, bring in that bottle. We've got words to say to it. Boy oh, boy, this is livin'!"

CHAPTER TWELVE

I T WAS AFTER six o'clock, and the sun was dying away in the smudge and smog of the late afternoon. Cecil had gone to the café, and Flossie and I sat alone, trying to talk me out of the gas chamber. We glared at each other and got ideas, saw them die under relentless pressure, shouted now and then, and paraded around the room. We looked like a writing team, trying to think up the theme for a million-dollar epic out of no plot at all.

Occasionally we lapsed into periods of glum silence only to have one or the other leap up and try to give birth to an idea. But we always stopped during the labor pains and said, "No, that's no good, because..."

None *were* any good. We were the Boy Scouts of America fighting Adolf Hitler's one-time Storm Troopers. We were not only bucking the syndicate, but also the smoothly turning wheels of justice. All of them, including the good citizens, thought that I had killed Moss. And you can't buy your way out of a bum rap unless you've got money. And don't tell me that some cops can't be bought. There are enough honest cops—almost. But that one word is what pays off for the Mosses and the Mannys.

I looked into my drink and shook my head.

"They've got me, Flossie."

"Feeling sorry for yourself, aren't you?"

I jumped up. "Sure! Who will if I don't? It's a cold world. Let's go eat, wha' say?"

"How about the girl friend you mentioned?"

I snapped my fingers. They didn't snap very well, and I felt foolish. "I'd forgotten about her."

"Just like a man. Can you call her?"

"Yes, there's a phone in the lobby, if the landlady will answer. Have you got time to come to our place for dinner?"

"Time's one of the few things I *have* got that Truman can't tax away. Sure she won't mind?"

"I'll call and ask her to put a few pots together. I don't suppose she's eaten yet."

"Is she fasting?"

"No, but she'll be worried about me."

Flossie snorted. "You men are so damned sure of yourselves!"

"Yeah, I guess you're right. I feel like a heel for not calling her."

She smiled. "Well, give her a buzz now, and if it's all right, I'll drive you over. I'd like to see a woman who's fool enough to fall for you—in your present fix. She must be an all-right gal."

"She is. 'Scuse me."

I called the place. The head keeper of Animal Flats grunted and turned away from the phone. Her mooselike bellow almost shattered my eardrums, and even Flossie jumped when she heard it from ten feet away. Doris' breathless voice answered, and I could imagine her slumping against the wall when she heard me speak. No, she hadn't eaten and would have dinner ready when Flossie and I arrived. I blew her a kiss and dropped the receiver in place.

Forty-five minutes later, Flossie had grimly bluffed her erratic way through the evening traffic. We trudged up the narrow, uncarpeted stairs and turned left down the dark hall, which was lit by a single weak, fly-specked bulb. I stopped at the end door and rapped softly. At once Doris flung it open and ran into my arms. She kissed me hard, then stepped back into the room and saw Flossie for the first time.

"Hello," she said. "I didn't mean to be rude, but I was *so* worried about Jack. Come in, Miss Narbonne,"

"You're helping him?"

"In a way. I'm a reporter."

Doris gasped. "A reporter!"

"Don't worry, honey, I won't chirp till everything's over and dead."

I couldn't help shuddering. Flossie smiled and patted me, then glanced around the room. I could see words lining themselves up in her mind, words that she would use later to describe our little hideaway. A mirrored portion of the wall hid the rollaway bed. There were two chairs, a divan whose cushions had been kicked up into three hard lumps, a scarred, ringed coffee table, and a floor lamp with one of those old-fashioned parchment shades with an early California painting on it. No carpet.

After the salad, hamburger patties, mashed potatoes, and peas, we sat in the breakfast nook sipping our coffee. Doris and I were on one side while Flossie lounged across from us, chain smoking. She spoke to Doris.

"You know Jack's in a spot, honey."

Doris nodded. "I wish I could do something about helping him."

"You can. Just keep him out of trouble while the real brains— me," she grinned, tapping herself on the chest, "can think of some way to get him out of his jam."

I growled at Flossie, then got three more coffee refills and a bottle of bourbon. Through two more pots of coffee royales we talked things back and forth, getting nowhere again. Doris' eyes got more worried, and at last she said:

"Flossie, what about Morrison's wife?"

Flossie shrugged. "I don't know the dame, but she can't be much good if she lived with him. He was the devil's personal emissary on earth."

"Wait a minute!" I protested. "That's a heck of a thing to say about a woman you've never seen!"

Flossie's eyes lit up eagerly. "In love with her, Jack?" She looked at Doris, then back at me. As she sat there, her mouth narrowed, her eyes alert, I could have killed her. I looked at Doris, who was suddenly interested in her coffee, out the window, and finally back at Flossie.

"Forget it, Jack," she said. "Stand on your constitutional rights. Well, I've got to go. It was a wonderful dinner, Doris. Call me sometime, Jack."

Doris was alarmed. "You're not going to help him?"

Flossie looked at Doris. "I shouldn't. Any man who's fool enough to be thinking of a woman like Moss's wife when he has you is just too damned dumb to live!" She turned to me. "Frankly, I don't like you, Jack. I think you're dealing Doris a bad hand. Anyone can see that Doris is mad about you. Nope, you're so stupid you don't deserve to live!" I started to get up, but she put a capable hand on my chest and shoved. I thumped down on the wooden seat and glared across at her. "You're no damned good, but I'm going to help you because I smell a whale of a story. That's why I'm sticking with you."

My lips twisted. "Get out of here!"

Flossie sneered. "Our little pride's hurt, isn't it?"

Doris placed a trembling hand on mine. "Don't, Jack. Please! Flossie, don't pay any attention to what he says. For God's sake, help him if you can. I'll be grateful forever!"

Flossie reached over and patted Doris' hand, being careful not to touch mine. "I will, honey. I like you for your guts." She slid from the booth, unfolded her long legs, and straightened up. "Jack, call me tomorrow. Good night, all," she ended cheerfully as she walked from the room. The front door slammed behind her, and I turned back to Doris.

"Old devil!" I muttered.

"Maybe so, but she can save your life, and you know it."

The next day I stayed in the apartment. I was sulking, and I was hoping Flossie would call. I had a caustic speech all worked up; it was a masterpiece, full of neatly turned phrases. Cecil called just once, and we talked for a few minutes till he sensed my feelings, then said good-by and quietly hung up.

Doris left me alone all day, calling me only for meals. That night I lay on the divan, working a crossword puzzle. My mind asked me, What's a four-letter word for fool, Jack? I snarled, "Are you asking, or telling me, Jumbo?"

I threw the paper on the floor and stared from the window into the night. If the Dark Angel of Death had fluttered up, poised on the window sill, then leaped for me, I wouldn't have bothered raising a hand to ward him off.

I looked across the room at Doris. She was curled up in a chair, watching me. Her face was filled with sadness. Something inside me said, Quit being a damned fool, Griffith! Get up, hold her in your arms, and apologize. You bastard, she's one woman in a million!

When I arose, she looked up, jumped to her feet, and met me in the middle of the room. She pressed against me tightly, and for minutes we stood, locked together. I looked down at her wavy red hair and smelled it, marveling again at the way it was always sweet and clean; no perfume, just her own special aroma. I tilted her head back and kissed her. Her eyes fluttered and closed at the same instant that her mouth opened, eagerly waiting. Finally I held her back.

"Sorry, baby, it won't happen again. I was just feeling sorry for myself, and you, too, maybe."

She looked up almost sadly. "Jack, don't you know that I always want to feel sorry right along with you, or happy, or anything else?"

"I don't deserve you, I swear I don't!"

She grinned. "Nope, guess you don't, but you've got me, red hair and everything that goes along with it." She looked toward the wall mirror. "And maybe you need me now—like I need you."

"It could be you're right. Let's find out."

But guess who I first thought of when Doris' arms opened up for me?

Yeah—guess!

We were lying close together. Doris' head was on the same pillow as mine, and she was breathing steadily in sleep. I looked down at her relaxed, pure face and brushed it with my lips.

Then someone knocked.

I cursed silently. Doris awoke and jerked erect in the bed, fright showing on her face like ugly streaks on a modernistic painting. "Sorry, baby. I'll see who it is. Yes?" I called.

It was the landlady, the haughty owner of Misery Manor. "Telephone!" she snarled.

"O.K., I'll be right out." I dressed and went below. She was waiting for me.

"I told you I don't like phone calls after nine o'clock. I had to get out of bed!"

I thrust my face next to hers and shuddered at the proximity. "So did I. We're even!" Her face reddened. "I'm sorry, Mrs. Platt. I'll try to see that it doesn't happen again. It must be about a job."

She mumbled something, and I went to the pay phone. The receiver was hanging, still swinging angrily.

"I'm here," I said cautiously.

"Jackie?"

"Hi, Cecil, what's the good word?"

The gay music rose and fell in the receiver as the laughter ebbed and flowed. "Guess who's here?" His voice was low, like a conspirator's.

"Mardi!"

"That's right. I just found out who she is. She wants you."

"Put her on!"

"No, I don't like it. It might be a frame."

"You're telling *me* about frames. I'm getting so I can sniff one out from the next block."

"But, Jackie! Think about me. What if—what if lots of things?"

"Yeah, I see what you mean, but I'll stake my life that she isn't working with the cops."

"You *will* be, doll," he murmured.

"Why'd you call me, then?"

"Because I knew you'd want to talk with her. All right, I'll do this much. I can keep myself more or less in the clear if I just intimate that you may be at a certain place, say tomorrow night. Other than that, I think I'd better keep out of it."

My brain cells danced for a few seconds. "Tell her I'll be at the Rocking Horse Grill, mustache and all, tomorrow night at eight o'clock."

"All right, but I don't like it. Not one little bit. Good luck!"

He hung up, and for minutes I stood there, leaning against the wall, studying the dirty plaster, thinking about Mardi, hating myself all the while, because upstairs was Doris, waiting for me, ready to put her warm arms about my neck and love me forever. But in the half darkness of the lobby, Mardi seemed to be with me; the past scenes we had together returned vividly to me. I walked up the stairs, getting a white lie together for Doris.

The Rocking Horse Grill. It's a whale of a place to take a date that you want to impress—if you're known there. They help you from your car and call you Mr. So-and-So, if you've tipped them enough before. The front door opens magically, and you are met by a smiling headwaiter and barbecue smoke.

Inside, the lights are dim, and you're back in Merrie England with vassals by the score to serve you. The talk is low, well mannered, and the women you see are more lovely than you can stand; they go with Brentwood homes and Cadillacs. Their men are there, and don't you try to make a pass unless you make three thousand a week. They are studio executives and directors, stockbrokers and bankers, with just a smattering of orchestra leaders and singers, eager starlets and their agents.

And you'd be surprised at how many people are told that they can't come in. "Reservations, booked solid for the night. Sorry, try the So-an-So across the street. Their food is—adequate." They turn away and feel sad, sensing the fact that they can't eat there because they don't complement the surroundings. And in bed that night, the wives cry a little because their Joes aren't respected.

But from the back, the Rocking Horse is not so impressive.

That was the way I came in to see Mardi. It was eight-thirty when I parked in back, next to the waiters' cars and the evil-smelling garbage-pails. Mine was one of the half-dozen parked cars, and blended well with the others. Not wanting to use Doris', just in case, and also because I had lied to her about going to meet Cecil, I had rented it from the owner's husband at Animal Acres. Twenty dollars had covered his expenses, and another twenty behind his wife's back had made his little eyes gleam and made us friends for life.

Just in case the Would You's? phone lines had been tapped, I stepped into the men's room and looked around. I felt better when L.A.'s Finest were missing from the scene. I stepped to the rear of the bar and ordered a double whisky, straight. The music was playing softly, and well-selected tunes drifted out from hidden speakers. I paid for the drink, lit a cigarette, and put the drink away where it belonged in a double swallow. I felt my mustache and hoped that it was a good disguise, at the same time knowing that Mardi would recognize me. Then I craned my head over the milling crowd.

My eyes traveled past the minks and ermines, expensive hair-do's and low-cut television gowns, around the room slowly, booth by booth, till I saw Mardi. She was so beautiful, I wanted to cry. She was sitting small and alone, with a Manhattan for her only companion, and she was watching it as if it was going to run away. Her fingers were curled tightly around the stem of the glass, her breath was jerky, and her facial muscles were tight like a violin string. I slid from the bar stool and stepped into the dining room.

The lips were the same ones that I had kissed and memorized, the body that strained against the gown was the one I had caressed, and the fingers that held the glasses were long and patrician. I was less than ten feet from her when her eyes smacked into mine. Her breath drew in, and she half arose. I motioned her back, shushed her with my fingers, and slid into the booth. Her body was warm against mine as I crowded her back into the shadows. Her lips parted, and one bare, trembling word slipped out.

"*Jack!*"

"Who'd you expect, dear heart—Manny?"

Her hand was shaking as she raised the glass, then her fingers fell apart suddenly, and the drink fell to the table. The glass shattered, turning everything into a spreading puddle, a red cherry, a few pieces of curved, broken glass, and a bare stem. She sank back against the booth, and I leaned toward her, trying to hold her up.

Then it happened.

Someone slipped into the booth next to me, pinning me against Mardi. My body went cold as my heart died inside me. Then cold hatred swept into me, and a new strength took over. My fingers gripped the cigarette by its glowing tip and crushed it without feeling the pain.

I turned away from Mardi, and before I looked, there was no doubt.

Lieutenant Grebel!

CHAPTER THIRTEEN

"HELLO, MAESTRO."

The room swayed out of focus, then came back to normal as I looked at Mardi. Her lips were moving silently and her face was a mixture of fear and pity. I smiled at her and turned to Grebel. His eyes were gloating. His mouth was a thin band, and the muscles in his neck were twitching. His hand was tensed inside his coat, and my eyes were hypnotized as they watched the little second hand move about the dial of his luminous watch. The tendons of his wrist jerked, making the short hairs jump nervously.

"Glad you could make it tonight, Griffith. We've missed you."

My eyes raised to his. "Yeah, I'll bet you have. You should live so long."

He tried a laugh, but it didn't fit his face, so he snarled. I turned my eyes back to Mardi for consolation. She shrank away, and in that instant something precious died inside me and I shook my head sadly. I looked at Grebel again and caught his eyes shifting foxlike from Mardi to me.

Then it was clear and cold like a cake of ice.

"Oh!" I breathed. "I get it now."

"What else?" Grebel said in a low whisper. "All right, let's go. We don't want a scene in here."

"Uh-uh! I won't buy that crate of apples. I like it here. It looks good, like a long life."

His hand was nervous inside his coat. "I don't want to kill you."

"Not in *here,* you mean! You'd love to see me dead. How else are you going to earn your keep? No, you won't kill me here, you'll wait till we're all cozy and alone. You don't fool me, Fish Face. You can't afford to have me live. Where's Manny—out in the hearse?"

"No, you funny bastard, he's home in bed, where all good citizens should be. Now, get up before I *do* kill you here!"

I saw a nervous movement over his shoulder and glanced up. Jackson, the headwaiter, was hovering just inside the circle of staring customers. I took a deep breath and motioned him over with a jerk of my head. He bounced up, his smile as nervous as a virgin on the verge, silently praying that no blood would be spilled on the Rocking Horse's expensive carpeting. He came up and recognized me.

"Yes, Mr. Griffith?" he said, swallowing his dryness.

"This—thing crashed my party, Jackson."

"But, Mr. Griffith, the police have been looking for you!"

"This dog isn't the police. He's a paid thug."

"Wait a minute, you brainy jackass!" Grebel roared.

As he turned toward Jackson, his gun hand shifted and reached inside to fish out his identification. That was the moment!

My hand had nervously been fingering the shaft of Mardi's broken glass stem. I raised it, measured the distance, and just before she screamed a warning, I slashed it across Grebel's face. With a roar of pain, he turned toward me. I dropped the bloody, jagged thing and poked two stiff fingers in his eyes. My fingers sank deep till they met his skull bone. The blood started flowing from his ragged cheek, and he fell blindly from the booth to the floor.

As she lunged toward me, I shoved Mardi backward. I leaped from the booth and brought my foot back, crashing it into Grebel's jaw. I loved the way his head flew back. The jaw dropped insanely open and the neck seemed to snap. Before any of the stunned patrons could move, I had reached down, picked his revolver from its trick holster, and was holding it hip high.

My hand swung around to cover the room. People shrank back. One dipso at the bar crossed himself and reached for his drink, his frightened eyes fixed on my mad face.

"If anyone moves, I'll shoot!" I screamed.

Grebel lay sprawled out on the floor like a worn-out sultana on a harem rug. I grinned almost happily. Jackson was the only one to protest as his Continental mind rebelled. "Mr. Griffith, I'll have to ask you to leave!" he cried.

I laughed. "I'm leaving, Jackson. Next time, save a booth for me—alone." I turned to Mardi, and love left me quickly, the way it had first come.

"You dirty bitch!" I snarled. "I ought to kill you!"

She shrank against the seat, her teeth biting into her clenched fist, her eyes starkly looking into mine. I raised the gun slowly and caught her in the web of the sights. She stared at me as I flicked off the safety, then screamed and fainted. She slumped into the darkness beneath the table, where only her white thighs were visible.

Would I have killed her if she had sat there, waiting?

I don't know. Guess with me.

I backed away slowly. A frightened waiter who had been standing motionless, fixed like a moth on a mounting pin, fainted as I neared him. His tray of barbecued spare ribs splattered on the floor. I bent down, picked one up, and gnawed on it, then threw it over the bar. It made a little smudge on the mirror. I wiped my mouth with my sleeve and realized that never before had meat tasted so good.

"I want just five minutes," I yelled at the gawking people. "If any man, woman, or headwaiter sticks his head out before then, they'll be grieved over. I didn't kill Moss Morrison, and I'm not going to die for what someone else did!" The grim humor of the situation suddenly hit me. "Jackson!" I called.

"Yes, Mr. Griffith?" he replied quietly, stepping forward slightly.

"I'm sorry that I ruined the trade for the evening. Really. Good night, all."

I backed out the door; I was the star of the evening, and in my third-act curtain, the eyes of the audience followed me, slowly and unwillingly. The bartender raised a bottle of whisky to his white lips and let the liquor gurgle into his willing stomach.

Somewhere behind me in the darkness, behind a wire fence, a dog barked.

"Quiet!" I roared. The dog kept on yelping.

Keeping the gun in my hand, I jumped in the car and stepped on the starter. It tried hard and seemed to be apologizing to me, but it couldn't turn over, as hard as it tried. For more than a minute I worked with it, praying harder than a Baptist preacher over sinning dancers.

I got from the car, holding the gun in front of me. Jackson's face peeked out. I waved the gun and he jumped inside, his hands nervously protesting before his head.

The Rocking Horse Grill was a good quarter of a mile from Washington Boulevard. I ran through the back streets, threw everything with one cast of the dice, and started thumbing.

The fifth or sixth car stopped to my frantic waving. I grinned and opened the door. He took me to La Brea, and then I struck off south and cut right into the hills, knowing that an alarm would even now be out for me. I climbed a fence, detoured around a lonely-looking house, whinnied back at an old, spavined horse, and started up the steep, bushy hill. The clay soil was slippery from the recent rains, and my feet kept slipping down, as if they were bent on dragging me to hell. But I managed to pull my way to the barren summit.

Half an hour later, I stood, a dark silhouette against the skyline, too tired and heartsick to care. Beneath me, miles to the south, lay Inglewood, and farther on, the beach cities. I sank down and covered my eyes.

Tears were slow in coming, but when they did, they burned my cheeks. My body trembled as it remembered Mardi's faithlessness. For long minutes I sat there till at last the tears were gone, replaced by a grim hatred.

Then I remembered something, and Doris' fear-haunted face cast itself before me. I had left the car behind, and they could trace it. They would go there, looking for me, and find Doris instead!

It took more than an hour to pick my running way down the hill and through ravines before I reached Centenila Boulevard. Three times I fell and rolled, sobbed with anger as I picked myself up, and ran again. As I neared the highway, I kept to the gulleys, and at last carefully peeked through the bushes at the streaming lines of cars that were slowly moving past me.

I looked fearfully down the highway. Half a mile to the right, a roadblock had been formed, and cars were being stopped. Cops were searching them, their flashlights sweeping through the front and back, then they were grudgingly being motioned on. To the left at the other intersection, another one had been formed.

Rat in a trap, without even a hunk of moldy cheese for the booby prize.

A hundred feet to the left, this side of the deadly intersection, an attendant was flicking off the service-station lights. On the near boundary of the lot was a pay phone station. I waited till he had ground off in his Model A, then slid down and crept to the phone, fishing for nickels and dimes.

The phone rang three times on the other end. I waited, crouched inside the booth, a bare two hundred feet from scowlingly efficient policemen. And then there was a noise on the other end as someone raised the receiver. I arose slowly.

"Yeah! Who's this?" a voice grunted.

I hung up without answering.

It was Manny Lewis!

I slumped to the floor of the booth and stared helplessly into the darkness. Everything that had happened before was a bad dream, but this capped things off neatly and turned the entire evening into a roaring nightmare. Manny had Doris; they had traced the car, then Manny had made tracks to South Gate.

I realized that I should have made a bargain with Manny to save Doris, but I had done the normal thing and hung up the phone. I got another coin out, and ten seconds later the phone was ringing again. This time, the female beast answered, jolting me, because I had expected Manny's gruff voice.

"Where's my—wife?" I demanded.

"The police took her. Where's our car?"

"You're worrying about a car when I've lost a woman!" I screamed. "Don't worry, you'll get it back and can charge money to let people sit in it. Who took her, a little fat fellow?"

"Yes, and four other policemen."

"Why didn't you ask to see their badges, goddamn it?" I roared. "He wasn't a cop any more than I am!"

"Look!" she screamed. "I didn't like you from the start, and I'm sorry we rented you the penthouse. I was against it, and I said—"

"What did this man say when he took her?" I interrupted.

"Nothing!"

"Did you see his car?"

"No, I went back inside, where I belonged. I don't mess in police things."

"All right, thanks, Mrs. Platt," I said, suddenly tired. I hung up quietly and slipped from the booth.

For a minute, I stood in the shadows, watching the road-block. The radio started blasting, and the cops started climbing back in their cars. I ran back in the hills and crouched behind the bushes, my eyes staring unseeingly at the sky.

Doris, forgive me!

Lord, how I needed a friend! I didn't deserve one, however, after the lie I had told Doris to get out to see Mardi, and after the fool I had been. I was a rat in one of those university mazes; every way I turned, I ran into a dead-end lane, and at each of the blank ends, the gas chamber waited.

My thoughts turned again to Doris and I prayed they wouldn't hurt her. I couldn't stand it. I loved her too much.

What was that, Griffith? You love her too much! Why, you damned fool, *you do love her!*

I thought of Doris' clean beauty and kind heart, tried to put Mardi's attributes on the scales next to them, and failed; Mardi's slipped off and fell into the mud. I looked straight ahead, tried to get used to the idea—then saw my capture staring me dead in the face.

Half a dozen prowl cars from the the two road blocks had pulled up on the boulevard less than fifty yards from where I sat hunched in the gully. I pulled the twigs aside and gasped. Get your guts together into a nice, tight cast-iron ball, Griffith. You're going to need them where you can find 'em in a hurry.

The police jumped from the cars, flashing their lights about absently. I let the cover slide back over me just as a powerful beam swung past the station and landed squarely on my hiding place. It lingered for a long second, and I almost died before it passed on. A sharp voice called the cops to attention and started giving orders. A tall man in an overcoat motioned with his hands toward my own personal hills and barked some more words.

I moved backward on my hands and heels as quietly as I could, creeping up the gully for a hundred feet, then turned over and scrambled up the side. The wet soil hid the noise as I moved up toward the brow of the hill, then cut right toward La Brea Avenue. I slid down the steep embankment, lost my footing, and rolled and tumbled and cursed, stopping only when I reached the bottom, behind a motel.

Through one of the windows, a shaft of light came. A young boy and girl were inside, and if I'd been her daddy, I'd have spanked her little rosy bottom for what she was getting ready to do. The boy was feverishly pulling the clothes from her body, biting on her naked shoulder. She squirmed happily and turned to face the raised curtain. At the sight of my twisted face, her mouth opened up, begging to scream. Twice it tried before a sound came out, then it made up for lost time as a shrill cry hit the night air. She fainted.

I raised the gun and held it on the boy as he fearfully turned around. He stood looking at me, his mouth open. Then his eyes rolled out of sight, his knees collapsed, and he sagged to the floor. The noise of his head hitting the foot of the bed made me grin happily.

In front of the cabin, his car waited, his own little six-cylinder chariot that was going to take him and Doll Baby to heaven's gates. I slid inside and felt in the darkness; the ignition keys were there, and I mentally thanked my own personal brand of luck. Things were looking up—like the unseeing eyes of an executed man. I let the car slide past the row of cabins, put it in gear, and felt the motor turn over and start.

So I was stealing a car? Well, I needed it more than he did right then, and he'd get it back. The radio had warmed up, and dance music came out slowly. I recognized it as my orchestra, the real thing, not records. You can always tell; the brasses sound stronger, and the piano has more tone. I listened through the program as I drove rapidly, passing cars cautiously after being sure that they didn't carry the insignia of Johnny Law. Then the program was over, and …

"Ladies and gentlemen" (Stealin' Smith was talking), "you have been listening to the music of Ronny Lund and his orchestra, coming to you direct from the world-renowned Psyche Ballroom, located in the heart 0f—"

My fingers killed the program, and I chuckled. So the bastard *had* changed his name and taken over, and now my name and future were both things of the past. It made sense, though. It wouldn't be good box office to have a murderer's name tacked onto the band.

I hit the back streets of Inglewood and crossed Manchester Boulevard. I headed south. I still hadn't seen any cops, but I kept to the back roads just in case, and I drove slowly, trying to think.

CHAPTER FOURTEEN

I T WAS A bright morning. The smudge was gone from the sky, and the air smelled clean. I had passed through the town of Orange, heading into the Santa Ana Canyon. When I was a kid, I had done a lot of shooting up there and knew the side canyons like my own secret thoughts.

On the left, in the valley, were acre after acre of orange trees, green and clean-looking. On the right were the low hills that stretched and reached out till they made their way back into the mountains.

The car grumbled and protested as I turned off the main highway onto a smaller, steep road, then onto a dirt road that led into Little Box Canyon, three miles back in the hills. The car barely made it in low gear and grunted thankfully when I ran it behind a final clump of scrub trees and switched off the ignition. After being sure that I was well hidden, I climbed wearily into the rear seat and slept the better part of the day away.

When I awoke, the air was sweet with the odor of the hills. I climbed from the car and stretched my aching body. Overhead, a few small birds fluttered from tree to tree. Higher aloft, in ever narrowing circles, a hawk soared, its wings motionless. Suddenly they folded, it dove for the earth, and some poor rabbit died by ripping talons and cruel beak.

The sun was slowly sinking behind the hills, and the shadows lengthened, long and purple. The birds were gone. Life stood still and made me want to pray. But I thought of only one thing— Doris' safety.

And then the nebulous first beginnings of a plan crept into my mind. They grew, swirled about, re-formed, and massed together till the plan worked itself up without my conscious help. I sat bolt upright and stared toward the Orion, high in the southern sky. It would work—or it would fail, but given half a chance before I died, I would turn Los Angeles upside down. And when my little effort was over, the town and the world might be a little cleaner.

No, it wouldn't be playing the game squarely, but that was for the boy scouts who had nothing more to lose than a merit badge. It would be dirty pool, nasty, bloody stuff, but it was the only way out. Only one route lay open.

I arose slowly and got into the car.

"Flossie?"

Her voice barely hid its dislike. "Where in hell have you been?"

"Still interested in the story?"

"It looks to me like the last paragraph has been written."

"Don't be so sure. I've got an idea."

"Treat it nicely. It's in a strange place."

"Go on, rub it in. I've got it coming."

"Just when I'm hating you, you get all nice and reasonable!" she complained. "All right, where are you?"

"Any chance you're being listened to?"

She paused. "No. The operator is busy with her knitting, and these lines can't be tapped."

"Fine. Come out to the One Hundred Café on the Pacific Coast Highway. It's east of Lomita about a mile."

"I know where it is. I'll be right out. And for God's sake, stay out of trouble!"

"For a change, I will. Make time!"

It was a dirty, crumby dive whose sign welcomed truck drivers. But it hadn't been a truck driver who put the lipstick on my coffee cup. I started to call the waitress over and complain about it, when I remembered another waitress that I had fallen in love with.

Doris baby, hold tight! Believe in me, I haven't forgotten you.

I rubbed the lipstick off and looked at the cherry-pink smudge on my finger. To save the girl some work, I took the empty cup to the counter for a refill and returned to my booth. I felt in my inner pocket for the snub-nosed revolver and felt a new strength.

An hour later, Flossie's maroon Cadillac convertible pulled up in front. The curb ticklers jingled merrily at me. She waved as she stepped from the car and was pulling off her gloves as she sat down.

"Hello, stupid," she said, sliding into the booth. I motioned the waitress for another cup of coffee.

"You really love to rub it in, don't you?"

"It isn't often that I meet the original damned fool and get the chance. Well, what about Doris?"

Yeah, what about Doris?

"Manny's got her."

"Tell me something I don't already know. He's made a deadline. Monday night you either give him your miserable carcass, or ..." The words died away in time with my heart.

"Will he do it?"

"You tell me. Personally, I think so. He's desperate."

"And this is Saturday. Why don't the cops do something?" I cried.

"Ask them."

"The dirty bastard, taking it out on a woman."

"You started it all when you had to see that Morrison bitch!"

"Where is she now?"

"I don't know. Probably either at her ancestral mansion on Sunset, or getting rates on the fare to hell. O.K., Brainstorm, let's have your hot idea."

The waitress got around to bringing the coffee, slopped some on the egg-splattered table, and spread the spill around with a dirty towel. I dropped a dime in her paw, curled my lip at her, and turned back to Flossie.

"You may not like it, but here goes...."

When I finished, it sounded pale even to me, and she shook her head sadly. "You poor misguided fool. You've got as much chance to get away with that as Il Duce did when the partisans caught him." She lit a cigarette and blew the smoke in my general direction. "But, as you say, there isn't anything else, and I haven't got a better idea."

I tried to smile. "How do you like your part in the little scheme?"

She shrugged. "You put me smack in murderers' row, but there's no point in living a hundred years just to make an ugly corpse."

"Got any boy friends you can trust?"

"I hate to admit it, but I've got a leg man."

"Will he help us?"

"He lusts after me, so I think he'll listen." She paused. "Take it easy, we've got company."

The waitress just couldn't stand it any longer. She had to see what the Cadillac convertible and the ill-clothed bum were gassing about. She stood at the end of the counter, idly brushing away nothing.

"Miss!" I called.

She looked startled and came over, her hips twitching angrily. "Yeah?"

"I know you were interested in what we were saying and couldn't quite hear, so I'll let you in on a secret. My mother and I are in love and want to elope, but our mean old grandfather ..."

She wheeled away, flushing, and I grinned at Flossie.

"You bastard!" she said. "*Mother!*" She smiled and picked up her gloves.

She squealed the tires in a quick turn, and as the powerful engine took over and pushed me against the seat, I closed my eyes. For some reason sleep came to me; the whirring of the car was a lullaby that kept me in dreamland till the car suddenly swerved.

"Damned fool," Flossie said, "turning without signaling!"

I looked up and saw the city hall in the hazy distance. My arms stretched, and I yawned. "My L.A.!"

"Yeah, there's no town quite like it—thank God," she said dryly.

Fifteen minutes later we were driving past the city hall. Over its main entrance, noble words stood out and eloquently proclaimed, "He that violates his oath profanes the divinity of Faith itself."

Flossie saw me reading it. "Nice words, aren't they?"

"Yeah. What do they mean?"

"Ask the politicians. I wouldn't know."

Ten minutes later she had pulled up in front of an ancient boardinghouse on top of Bunker Hill. One of the safest places to hide was there; people minded their own business, because it didn't pay not to. It had three stories and was top-heavy in its narrowness. Beneath it was a cheap café, dark inside with greasy smells floating out.

I looked at the grim building, then back at Flossie. "Is it safe?"

"From earthquakes, I don't know. About your miserable life, what have you got to lose? Sure, it's safe, or I wouldn't have brought you here. They won't know you, and there won't be any questions. Besides, I own it."

"*You?* I didn't know you were a broker."

"I'm not. The place was willed to me during prohibition by an old admirer."

"You know the *nicest* people, Flossie. Let's go up, if the stairs won't cave in."

She put me in the front room, overlooking the dirty street, leered at the manager, and left. I watched her out-of-place Cadillac pull away from the curb, then flopped on the lumpy mattress and played with the gun. I slept fitfully, and it was late afternoon before Flossie returned. I was nervous and restless, and I needed some fresh air.

CHAPTER FIFTEEN

LOSSIE AND I drove to an obscure drinking place on Santa Monica Boulevard. I sat down at the bar, while she went to the phone booth. She was in there long enough for me to have two slow drinks. I could see her angry gestures, and I knew she was having trouble. She was talking to Manny Lewis.

At last she came out of the booth and sat down on the stool next to me. She reached for the drink I had ordered for her and downed it in a gulp.

"What did Manny say?" I asked fearfully.

"He'll be there tomorrow night, Sunset and Vermont at eight o'clock. I threatened to publish the whole story in my column. But, as I thought, he won't bring Doris. He promises to let her go when you give up the fight."

"His promises mean as much as a politician's."

"Are you sure you want to go through with it?"

"What else can I do? They've got Doris."

She looked at me closely. "Maybe you've got more guts than I gave you credit for."

"I'm just getting senile, that's all. Are you sure your leg man won't let you down?"

"He'd better not. I've made him a promise that I want to keep." She leaned toward me. "If you weren't such a jerk and didn't have such a nice girl, I'd do big things to you."

"Yeah, but I am, and I have. All right, let's you take me back to my little Bunker Hill nest. And don't forget you're going to have a car there for me tomorrow night."

She sighed, and we left.

The next day I stayed in the room. I had some sandwiches and coffee sent up, and I gnawed on my fingernails.

At six o'clock I went out. In front of the place, just like Flossie had promised, there was a car. I whistled; she had really gone overboard. It was a year-old Oldsmobile, nice and shiny, a four-door sedan. With all that engine behind me, I couldn't lose.

Or could I?

Manny's fortress was on the north side of Wilshire, west of Beverly Glen in the Bel Air district. I parked between street lights and shifted the side mirror so that I could watch his imported pebble-stone driveway. I sat there, smoking cigarettes and drinking canned beer that I had thoughtfully picked up at a liquor store. An hour later, a pair of headlights flashed from behind the shrubs and dipped gently as the car bounced onto the street and turned east. I tossed the last empty can on the floor, waited till the bulletproof Cadillac whipped past me, then switched on the engine and took off after it.

The car was full of Manny and his thugs, and I kept it in sight, following behind the taillights at a safe distance. We passed Fairfax Boulevard, then Western Avenue, and my breath caught high in my chest and wouldn't let go. At Normandie, the traffic slowed down, and I saw a '40 Chevie pull away from the curb. The older car passed me, a hand waved, then the driver bent low over the wheel and shot forward.

As it pulled parallel to Manny's car, the driver blasted with his horn, swerved right, and crashed into the left front wheel of Manny's car, crippling it. I hoped. The racket of the two cars' mating was terrific, coupled with the other screeching brakes. The following drivers pulled away in a hurry like good citizens so they wouldn't be called as witnesses in a damage suit. I stopped twenty feet behind the wreck, switched off my lights, and waited.

Manny's bodyguards jumped from the car, their hunched, bull shoulders belligerently thrust forward, their faces tense.

The other driver said something to them and slowly pulled away out of the traffic lane to the curb, deliberately leading them a good fifty feet in front of the wrecked Cadillac. The thugs trotted after him. I waited till they were poking their heads in his window, each wanting to make a good show with Manny. Then I slipped from my car and walked ahead.

I opened the rear door and hopped in. Manny looked up, and sheer fright replaced the anger on his pasty face. "Hello, Manny. Remember me?" I asked him.

He sank back, unbelievingly, then leaned forward and started to yell. I whipped the revolver from my pocket and slammed it against his nose. He whimpered and felt the pulpy mass.

"One croak, Frog Face, and you die. Let's go!"

He started to speak, changed his mind, and said, "It won't work, Griffith."

All I said was: "After you, baby." He hesitated. "Manny, I'll kill you while you're sitting here if you want it that way. So help me Hannah, I mean it!" He shook a little. I opened the rear door on his side, then looked at the other car. Manny's boys were cursing Flossie's leg man, and one of them reached inside to grab him. Manny's feet were uncertain, slow-moving things as he stepped onto the pavement. I jammed the cold muzzle of the gun against his neck, and he stepped faster.

"That's right, Manny. You'd look simply ghastly without a head. How would they bury you?"

In the street, he tried to turn left up on the sidewalk. I herded him back with the gun and got a look at his drawn face. Fright was etched into every line, and his muscles were sagging, making him look like the oldest man in the world.

"Step it up!" I snarled.

He jumped ahead nervously. I opened the rear door to my car and shoved him inside, then slid in front and wriggled behind the wheel. He sank back in the seat, staring blankly at the floor. Guts? Not Manny. He could dish it out, but he couldn't take it.

I raised the gun by its barrel and brought it crashing down against his head. He gave a little sigh and slumped to the seat. I pulled him forward, heard him fall in a fat plump on the floor, then started the car and slid it into gear. When I drew even with the leg man, I gave the horn two quick beeps. He gunned his car and took off, spraying thugs like tenpins.

The last glimpse I had in the rear-view mirror showed a jumping bunch of thugs waving their fists, a couple of them reaching into their coats, three rapid shots, then no more. I cut south on Vermont and slowly worked my way through dark streets to Bunker Hill. I was careful, wanting to attract an eager traffic cop about as much as I wanted Manny to die—then.

He was still a cold sardine when I went upstairs to clear the coast. The hall was as dead as usual. I went into my room and everything was as I'd left it. I made double time down the stairs to the deserted street. Manny was the original sack of potatoes when I lugged him from the back seat. I tried to carry him, but he slipped from my arms and fell, striking his head on the sidewalk. Then I got smart, brought him to his feet, threw one of his fat arms over my shoulder, and staggered up the stairs.

It took five minutes to get him to my room, and I sighed happily when I dropped him on the bed. I dragged up a straight chair, took off his shoes, and lit a cigarette. His pudgy face was baby-like, smooth and powdered, sleek with success. He groaned again, and the time had come to snap him out of his reverie. I took a final drag on the cigarette, and as the smoke poured from my nostrils, I ground the cigarette into the sole of his bare foot. I picked a shred of tobacco from my mouth as I watched the burning coals fall to the floor.

He came to, screaming. I raised my fist high and drove it into his jaw. This time I let him come to by himself, and when he did, he was a quiet believer. I ripped a gag from the worn sheet on the bed, stuffed it into his mouth, and tied it. He was conscious when I sat down, and his eyes were beady little things that hated me. Tough.

"Remember me, Mr. Big?" I asked.

When he tried to sit up, I brought the revolver from my pocket and held it in my lap. "Relax," I said. He sank back, his bugged-out eyes watching the gun. "I've got some questions to ask you, and I've got a lot of time to wait for the right answers. And when I take off that gag, you're goin' to talk, sing, chirp like a little yellow canary. Why? 'Cause if you don't, you sleazy little bastard, I'm going to work you over from stem to stern!" My voice was rising, and I had to work to force it down. "I know a lot of tricks, nasty ones that not even you have ever heard of. When I get finished, you're going to pray for death like you've never prayed before.

"You think I'm kidding, baby? Uh-uh. The most hard-up mortician in the world is going to throw up when he sees what he's got to work on. You made a bad mistake, Manny. You picked the wrong man to cross up. You thought I was a soft push-over, a sissy-pants orchestra leader. Well, maybe I was, but in the last couple of weeks, I've remembered some of the things I learned during the war. And now I'm tough, Manny, real tough. You wanted to kill Moss. That was O.K., maybe he had it coming. But you shouldn't have tried to frame me for the job. I don't like bum raps. I'm too restless, it makes me all nervous inside.

"I don't want you to talk yet, so don't worry about the gag. I want some fun. God knows I've got it coming, and He's not going to blame me for collecting it. You ruined my life, and I'm going to get all the pay checks, dollar by dollar, out of your greasy little hide."

He groaned, and sweat bloomed on his forehead. A vein started to throb in his temple, continued on down his neck, then disappeared into his shoulder as it gushed toward his heart to get a recharge for another fearful round trip. His eyes were staring, as vacant as an empty store window. He looked around the room as if he were expecting a special friend to open an exit for his escape.

I grinned. "Look good, Manny, because you won't be seeing anything after I get through with your eyes. I learned a little trick in Italy—a needle in each eyeball, deep, then another one till—"

His eyes had rolled upward out of sight, and his fat head drooped to one side. His mouth sagged open.

The poor little devil had fainted. I guess he knew that I meant it.

For the next grunting, sweating ten minutes, I undressed him down to his brightly designed silk shorts. I spread-eagled him on the bed, tying him with the rest of the sheet, then stood near the head of the bed and started playing bombardier with lighted matches on his hairy chest. He came to, screaming through the gag. Then he closed his eyes, waiting for each match to fall. By midnight all the matches were gone, and I didn't want to run out and get more. I took off his gag, and his face was a messy fright as he silently watched me.

"Thirsty, Manny?"

He nodded pathetically.

"That's tough!" I snarled. "You'll be lots thirstier in hell this time tomorrow."

"Jack, please!" he wept.

"Where's my girl?"

"I don't know."

"You took her. Talk, and fast!"

"I swear I don't know!"

"O.K., Manny. As I told you, I'm really not in any hurry."

He wanted to scream, but nothing but little trapped squeaks came out. "Jack—love of..."

"Mr. Griffith, punk. Let's hear you say it as if you loved the word."

"*Mr.* Griffith, I don't know. On the grave of my grandmother, I swear!"

"Your grandmother died in a kennel. Does Grebel have the girl?"

His eyes got crafty. "That's it. He's got her—at his house."

"You lie in your teeth. He wouldn't take the chance. Where'd you hide her?"

He was quiet.

It didn't take much to put him out. I merely took the gun and tapped his head lightly. It didn't even break the skin. I replaced the gag, checked the knots that held him, and left the room.

I was hungry.

I ate in the cockroach palace beneath the place, then went to the phone in back and called Flossie. She answered and seemed a little flustered. It was easy to imagine her fixing up her rumpled hair while she talked.

"Did I interrupt anything, Flossie?"

"You picked a hell of a time to call," she said in a low voice. "Do you have him?"

"Yeah, I'm working him over, so you'd better come up and get a ringside seat. The show is continuous, main feature showing again in half an hour."

"I'll be over after a while."

"I see what you mean. Well, go back to—work and come when you can. I'm sorry if I spoiled anything." She grunted something nasty and slammed the phone down. At the corner drugstore, I bought a small packet of needles and thread and walked back to the place, humming like a happy damned fool.

Manny was awake and squirming, trying to break loose from his bonds. I tickled his ribs heavily with the gun and his body slumped back to the mattress. His eyes got that look again that I really hated to have to see—the cornered-animal stare.

"Feel like telling your old Uncle Dudley, Manny?"

He tried to speak again, the grunts protesting his lack of knowledge.

"All right, Act Two, Scene One. Blind Man's Buff." I took the needles out and stuck them in the mattress slowly so that his wide eyes could follow my every move. I showed him the thread. "After I'm through with you, I'll sew your eyes shut so the light won't hurt your blind spots." I roared with laughter and rocked back and forth more than I really felt like doing.

"The first ones are going to hurt, something terrible, and you'll think that the front of your head is exploding. That's what a blind beggar in Rome told me once. And he says that you can't faint, because the nerve centers won't let you. But that's not so bad, because the next needles actually blind you. He told me that."

Manny's eyes were bulging, trying to escape from their sockets. I picked up a needle and wet it with my lips. "I guess it's not very sanitary, but it's not going to make much difference an hour from now."

I slowly started it moving toward his right eye. He thrashed wildly, and without even taking my intent eyes from the job at hand, I picked up the gun and held it to his temple.

"Hold still, Manny. This is your big scene. Second-act curtain!"

His fascinated eyes followed the shiny needle till they crossed, and finally through the gag he screamed. His eyes pleaded; they would have done anything for me.

I stuck the needle back in the mattress and took off his gag. "Talk. This is your last chance. And if you think I'm playing, try me out!"

"She's—with some of my men," he gasped. He saw my face and said without taking a breath, "She's safe, they won't hurt her."

"They'd better not! Where is this place?"

"I . . ." I jammed the snub-nosed revolver into his fat stomach and saw it bury itself deep into the layers of fat. He winced and breathed deeply a few times, then muttered, "Thirty-five-ninety-two McClintock."

I sighed and let out a deep breath that had been caught in my guts. "Thanks, Manny. I guess I ought to kiss you."

He was suddenly brave. "You'll never get her, Griffith. They got orders to kill her first!"

I leaned over him, my face almost touching his. He shrank away as I said, "Manny, if they've harmed her, if they've even thought about it, I'm coming back here and kill you. So help me God, I mean it!"

He knew that I did, and turned his suddenly white face away.

I called Flossie again. This time her voice was friendly, and she was purring like a cat.

"Hello, Jack. Glad you called. What's new?"

"Is your leg man there?"

"It's just possible. What do you want him for?"

"Will he guard Manny? I found out where Doris is hidden."

"Good for you, boy. Hold tight, we'll both be over."

I ordered a hamburger for Manny. While the waiter watched goggle-eyed, I opened it, spilled half a shaker of salt on it, smiled at him, dropped a quarter on the counter, and walked out whistling.

CHAPTER SIXTEEN

MANNY WAS GRATEFUL and gulped down the salty hamburger without a whimper. He wiped his fat mouth with the hand that I had freed.

"Thirsty, Manny?"

"Yeah, I could sure use some."

"O.K., I'll do that much for you, and then we're going to do some more talking. I've got lots of questions." I got the water and had to make three more round trips before I straddled the chair and sat down facing him.

"Now, where does Mardi fit into this pretty little picture?"

He whitened. "Don't let's go into this thing again!" he pleaded. "You got what you wanted."

"Only part of it, buster. It isn't every day that I get such a neat doublecross from a woman. Where is she now?"

He shook his head. "I can't tell you any more. I'd get rubbed out."

"It's better to die like a man than meet the devil as a driveling idiot. I haven't even started to work on you."

"God, Jack, you ain't human!" he sobbed.

"No? And who the hell made me into the beast that I am? You guys did, all three of you. *Wait* a second, I'm just beginning to get the setup. What's Grebel's cut of this new deal? It's bound to be more than just bribery."

He shook his head. My hand flashed up, and he was too late in trying to ward off the blow. My open palm ached from the impact, and I sat rubbing it, waiting for Manny to quit choking.

His head finally rolled to one side, and he whimpered. I pulled his head back.

"What does Grebel get out of this?"

Manny shook his head. "Manny, I'll *really* work you over this time, and I won't be so nice about stopping when you want to talk. And you will, because you can't help it. You're yellow, and you can't stand pain. Now, save yourself!"

"What do you want to know?"

"Grebel's racket. All of it!"

"He's got a cut in L.A. He's our 'in' man at headquarters."

"Uh-*huh*, very neat. You just can't lose with a connection like that. Now, how about Mardi? Was she out after Moss's fortune, or does it go deeper than that?"

Manny bit his lip till the blood oozed out and shook his head. I raised my hand, and he croaked:

"She's married to Grebel!"

"Married! When?"

"Nineteen-forty-two."

"Nineteen … That dirty bitch! Did Moss know? I didn't need to ask that question, did I, Manny? The night you killed Moss, did she know about the frame-up?"

He nodded wearily. "Yeah, she knew."

"Why did you kill Moss? Had you been cheating on him, or did you have plans that he didn't fit into?"

"Moss had to die so's we could take over. That bastard was getting all the gravy and was set to live forever. I figured they'd put me in charge out here, and they did." His eyes lit up, proud-like. Mr. Big Shot—lying tied to a dirty mattress.

"And you guys picked on me, because you had to have a good, tight motive. I was pretty well known, and the syndicate boys wouldn't look past my dead body."

"Somethin' like that, I guess."

"Who master-minded this?"

"Grebel and Mardi."

"And now your little trio is riding high. You'll *really* be able to chisel now, won't you?" I shook my head sadly. "Only you won't, Manny. They'll take over."

"Whatcha mean?" he cried. His face was alarmed. He didn't get it.

"You don't know? I've got to kill you, Manny."

"God, Jack, don't talk like that!"

"Sorry, but it's you or me. There'll be one down and two to go."

His voice was croaking, and his face made me want to turn away.

"Jack, I'll do anything," he babbled. "Whatever you want is yours. I'll give you a cut out of the Pacific Coast section, I'll do anything. Whatever you want. Only for the love of God, don't kill me!"

"It's nothing personal, Manny," I said softly.

His free hand started clawing at my chest. I pushed it away and got up to lean over him. His eyes were streaming tears, and his face was tightly drawn.

"How do you want it, Manny? In the stomach?"

And then he was silent, and I thought he had fainted again. I looked at him closely and raised his eyelids. His eyes were glassy. He was barely breathing, and his lips were moving silently. Then I knew that he was praying and for a second I felt sorry for him. I put my hand on his forehead; it was death-damp cold. I retied his hand as his praying went on unheeding.

A woman's rapid footsteps sounded on the stairs. I got up, crossed the room, and switched off the light. The footsteps stopped outside, and there were three soft knocks.

"Flossie?" I whispered.

"That's me. Open up!"

I opened the door and pushed her back into the darkness of the hall. "There's no reason for Manny to see you," I said. "I wouldn't give two cents for your life if he ever got away."

We sat on the top step of the landing and talked in low tones. Then she asked the question that I most feared to answer.

"How are you going to get Doris? You'll have less chance than a Republican at Fort Knox."

"I know it, so guess who's next? Grebel, or someone else like his wife. Where does he live?"

"That big mansion out on Adams. Thirty-one-ninety-two West, to be exact. But you'll never get him that way. He'll know that Manny's gone by now and will be expecting you."

"We'll see."

"You're flippin' your cork, boy. A little bit of success has gone to your head."

"Make a bet? I've got four bits that says Mardi's either at her place or Grebel's, probably his. You see, they're married."

"Married!"

I told her the story, and she shook her head. "I want to throw up, Jack."

"I know what you mean. Anyhow, during these trying times, she'll more than likely be with her husband. I'm going out and get her while he's out on the original wild-goose chase."

Even in the darkness I could feel Flossie shudder. "I'd hate to have you after me, Jack. You hate hard, don't you?"

"Damned hard! I've got to, because the harder I hate, the more of them I can kill before they kill me. I don't expect to live through this, but I'm going to make my death count for something other than worm feed."

Her hand fell to my shoulder. "Good luck, Jack. You'll be needing it. Now, what can I do?"

"Where's the leg man?"

She lit a cigarette and grinned. "Downstairs."

"Do you like him?"

"I've been passing up a bet. We'll get along. You want him to watch Manny, is that right?"

"Yeah, and if you've got any vacant rooms, reserve one for the next paying guest."

"I always keep a couple of spare rooms for my stories. It'll be the rear one on the left."

"Good. Don't rent it till you hear from me."

"You've got guts, Jack," she said. "I take back what I once thought about you. But what about little Doris?"

"I'm gambling. It's like trying to make a point the hard way when you've only got one more throw. I don't want to stage a big fat rescue unless I have to." I stood up. "I'm leaving now. Say, where'd you get the Olds?"

She shrugged. "Heck, I bought it. You needed a car, I needed a story, I couldn't lose. I can always sell it when this is over—if you don't get blood all over the cushions."

"Flossie, if it isn't my blood, I'll be glad to buy new seat covers. Carry on, doll. I'm riding tonight!"

I pulled to the curb at the corner of Santa Monica and Western and walked into a drugstore to use the phone. An elderly druggist looked up hopefully from his seat at the closed soda fountain and went back to working his crossword puzzle when I pointed to the phone booth. I fished out a nickel and dialed the Would You? Café. As before, Cecil answered.

"Cecil, you know who."

"Hi, doll. Still love me?"

"More than ever. Will you do me a favor?"

"Name it."

"What's the name of that bar a block south of yours?"

"The Royal Club. It's strictly from hunger, you wouldn't like it."

"I'm not going there. But I'd like *you* to, and let me call you in five minutes."

"Sure," he said, getting the idea—tapped wires that lead to execution. "Five little old minutes."

"Thanks." I hung up and watched the second hand glide around the radium dial five times. I gave him an extra thirty seconds, but it had been wasted. Before the phone rang once completely, he had picked it up. His voice was lower, and I almost didn't recognize it.

"Royal Club. Phoebe speaking."

"Hi, Phoebe, this is Mandrake, the Dead Duck. Can you afford to help me?"

"What *can't* you afford to do for a friend? What gives, Jackie?"

"The beginning of the end, or something like that. In thirty minutes, *not* before, call up Grebel and tell him that you've got news about Manny. Tell him he's being held on the third floor of a hotel on Second and Main Street. You might dicker with him first, then agree to wait till tomorrow to contact him about a pay-off. Tell him your name's—uh—Young. Then hang up."

"Is that all? Couldn't I try to date him?"

"Lay off him, Cecil. He's poison from the word cyanide. Will you do it?"

"You knew I would, or you wouldn't have called me. How's everything coming?"

"I'll tell you in hell. *Adios, amigo.*"

"*Auf Wiedersehen, mein Schatz.*"

It was one of those older houses, built when the street was the chi-chi place to live, like Brentwood is now. It stood on the corner, high above the street, proud and aloof, sneering down at the passing parade. It had memories, glorious ones of the past, carriages and proud black horses, gracious ladies and gallant gentlemen, huge parties, champagne, and good living.

Now a cheap grafter lived in it, and the house, knowing it, must have been ashamed. I parked my car half a block west on Adams and stood leaning against the lamppost at a bus stop. A light shone through the curtained windows, casting two shadows on the curtain. Two silhouettes were walking back and forth jerkily, like puppets in a crazy dream, and it was easy to know who they belonged to. Mardi and Grebel. I spat into the darkness of the street, but the ugly taste remained in my mouth.

Suddenly the shadows stiffened and froze, then disappeared. I knew that Cecil was talking to Grebel now. I tried to light another cigarette, but my hands were shaking, and I threw it away unlit. I had to step back when the grinding noise of a bus approached. I motioned the driver on and looked at the people all cozy and warm inside. I started getting that desolate, all-empty feeling that had been my companion for so many days. But when I reached down and patted the revolver, I felt better, and I shifted my position against the lamppost.

At that instant a car roared from the driveway, catching me by surprise. Just as the headlights raked through the night, I stepped behind the lamppost, still watching the car. He wheeled east on Adams; his shoulders were hunched over the wheel, and his head was jutted forward, urging the car on.

As soon as the taillights disappeared, I double-timed it back to my car and tore away from the curb. I shot up the driveway, scraping the front bumpers on the cement, slammed to a stop, and ran noisily for the door. I turned the knob. The door was locked, and I banged three times. Mardi's rapid footsteps crossed the kitchen floor, and she said softly:

"Honey?"

I covered my mouth with my hand and muttered, "Yeah, open up, somethin's gone wrong."

The door flew open and I jumped inside, slamming it behind me. Her face couldn't believe it. She backed across the room, a veined hand across her mouth. She wheeled about and ran for the stairway, but one lunge made her my prisoner. I dragged her to me till our mouths were almost touching.

"What's the matter? I thought you were mad about me. C'mon, I want a kiss!"

Her features were suddenly uglier than a Halloween mask. Her arms flew upward and pushed me. She jerked free and ran for the stairs again. This time she was halfway up before I caught her by taking them three at a time. With one final jump, I made it and caught her by the right shoulder.

She flew back, lost her footing, and fell past me. Her head hit the railing, her mouth sagged open, and she fell down the carpeted stairs. I followed her to the bottom, looked down at her unconscious body, then picked her up and carried her to the huge sofa in the living room. Her head hung loosely back, and her face was relaxed. For the first time I was able to see her as she really was, nasty, and yet very, very beautiful.

As I let her drop from my arms, her head flopped sideways on the cushions, and she stirred. I sat smoking while her breathing gradually caught hold and came back to normal. She opened her eyes, and I blew two lungfulls of smoke into her eyes. She blinked, softly at first, then the tears came, and if I hadn't been such a dirty dog, I'd have been touched.

I laughed.

She wiped the tears away, and her mouth drew back over her teeth like a caged tigress.

"What do you want here?"

"What do you *think* I want? I came back to find something I lost. My heart. It's somewhere inside that pretty body, and I'm going to operate on you, bone by bone, till I find out where you've hidden it."

I took the gun from my pocket. "Recognize it? It's your husband's, your lover's. God!" and the shudder that swept through me was real; I was suddenly cold. "Yours must be a great love, married to one man, then another at the same time. And I'll give you five to three you'd have married me too if it would have helped you any."

She pushed herself up from the divan and walked toward me slowly, half crouching. Her eyes were afire, and her fingers were talons as she made her way silently, like a jungle animal. I tossed the gun across the room and waited for her. Feet away from me, she suddenly grabbed a large glass ash tray from an end table and threw it. I leaped aside, shielding my face, and dropped down. The thing shattered a mirror over the fireplace, and the slivered glass fell to the floor, grating beneath my feet as I moved toward her.

My fist opened up and slapped her face, reversed itself, and with all of the pent-up fury in my body caught her on the other cheek. She fell back against the end of the divan, her hands on her marked cheeks. I went to her and jerked her erect. I looked deep into her flashing eyes.

"Yeah, I came back. To collect!"

My mouth swooped down to cover hers, but the love had been replaced by something deeper, more primeval. It was a thing remote from my mind, a hating gesture meant to hurt, maim, conquer. The kiss was long and hard, and our teeth grated together.

Her arms, which had been hanging loosely by her sides, slowly crept up around my shoulders, then my neck, holding me in a vise. Her breasts surged against me, and her mouth opened. Then she sank her sharp teeth into my lower lip.

The pain blinded me, and I tried to shake her from me. But her fire held me in bondage, and her teeth sank deeper till they met. I drew back my fist and buried it in her stomach. She sank back and fell to the floor. As I stood looking down on her, the taste of my own blood was satisfying.

She looked up. Her teeth were bared, and her breathing was fast.

Her tongue slowly licked her lips, and her eyes narrowed with lust and hatred. She moved her hands down slowly and raised her dress. There was in the wanton gesture an eternal promise. Her smooth thighs belonged to me, and they were suddenly very desirable.

I stared at her. My thundering heart and taut body said they wanted her, but my lips said, "Go to hell!"

She jumped up screaming and lunged for me. She ran straight into my crashing fist. I caught her before she fell, threw her over my shoulder, and walked toward the door. Barely feeling her weight, I stooped, picked up the gun from the floor, and carried her toward the car. Once I looked down, and her mouth was open like a woman being loved.

I dumped her in the back seat, tore her skirt and made a gag from it, stuffed it into her mouth, and tied her hands behind her body. She was lying face down on the rear seat, but when I backed into the street, she rolled forward and fell on the floor, where she lay whimpering. I didn't bother to look around.

The car slid to a stop in front of Flossie's rooming house. I got out, stretched idly, and looked up and down the street. Everyone was in bed, dreaming the only dreams they ever had. I opened the rear door of the car, reached inside, and picked up Mardi.

I threw her over my shoulder, and in three running steps reached the sanctuary of the stairs. I passed Manny's private room and walked to the end of the dark hall. Flossie opened to my knocking, saw Mardi hanging over my shoulder, and chucked her under the chin.

"Hello, dearie. Come in and give your old Auntie Flossie an exclusive interview. She just adores talking to the other—the *lower* half!"

CHAPTER SEVENTEEN

W E TIED Mardi to a straight chair in the middle of the room. Her face was twisted into something ugly, resembling a woodcut out of Grimms' fairy tales, the bad witch in the Black Forest. As I stood looking down on her, my eyes reflecting the pain in my soul, she seemed to change. Gradually the hatred left her face, and she wilted, like a rose that has lain too long on a tombstone.

"Watch her," I told Flossie. "Don't untie her for any reason."

"You're leaving now?"

"Yes. And if anything goes wrong …"

"Just what the devil *will* I do if anything goes wrong? All I've got is your word about this whole stinking mess. Jack, if something goes sour, they'll throw me so far in the dungeon I'll *never* see the sun again!"

"Want to leave?" I asked her softly.

My teeth must have gleamed, because she shuddered. "Not when you look at me that way. Oh, so what? I've always wanted to do a feature article on Tehachapi Prison."

"That's swell. Stick with me, and maybe your dream will come true. Talk with her all you want to, and if she makes a fuss, slap her silly."

Thirty-five-ninety-two McClintock was the last house in the block. It was a tall place, two storied, with another half story perched on top, setting off the gingerbread that trimmed it. It might have been any of the thousand rooming houses for the college kids at U.S.C.

Or it could have belonged to an old woman who lived there with pictures of her dead husband, sitting alone and eating cold beans because her pension check was a day late. It could have been any one of those, but it wasn't. The two late-model cars that stood in the driveway, the class of cars that were bought with racket and blood money, told me that there wasn't any doubt. I recognized the one parked nearest the street; it belonged to Grebel.

I parked around the corner on a dark street where I could watch the place, turned off the lights, and waited.

Ten minutes and two cigarettes later, Grebel walked out, his jaw jutting in front of him. He looked about and hitched his top-coat higher, then climbed into his car and drove away.

I switched on my lights and turned on the ignition. I turned west on the next street. He stopped at a drugstore and came out half a minute later, his nervous fingers ripping the cellophane from a package of cigarettes. I followed him till I knew he was going back home, then I circled back toward the house on McClintock, stopping first at a filling station to use the phone. I gave him fifteen minutes, then dialed his number. He answered on the first ring, and his voice was the tightest thing I had ever heard.

"Mardi!" he yelled. "Where the devil you been?"

"Just call me Jack for short. How are you feeling, Grebel?"

"Griffith! Where are you?"

"Oh, around, somewhere in town, I guess. Isn't Mardi there?"

"Mardi!"

" 'Scuse me, Mrs. Grebel, I mean. I hear that you two have cooked up a lovely romance over the years. Very touching the way you took Moss to the cleaners. Pitiful thing about that. Even if he can talk God out of a sentence on the rackets, he'll have to take a bum rap on an adultery charge. Won't that be hell?"

"You funny bastard!" he snarled.

"Yeah, I knew you'd see the humorous side of it. Oh, I happened to remember something. Mardi and I went for a ride together, and she won't be back for a while. Maybe never!"

His voice dropped, but it was powerful and threatening. "Where is she, Griffith?"

"You tell me something. Where's Doris? Where's anyone during these trying times?"

"What's your deal, Griffith?"

"You know damned well what it is. A trade, even Steven, straight across the board." I held my breath for his answer, and when he said:

"Go to hell!"

I almost did.

"Maybe I will, Grebel, but I'm going to drag you right along with me. All right, you louse, you won't deal?"

"Not worth a damn, unless you throw Manny in, too."

"I'd love to, but he's dead," I lied. "I killed him less than an hour ago. Do you want his corpse?"

"So you're the dirty ape who sent me on that chase!"

"None other. Well, if that's the way you feel, I'll go ahead with Alternate Plan B. I've got nothing to lose if I kill that slut you call your wife. Want to change your mind?"

"No!" he screamed. "There isn't a woman in the world who's worth what I stand to lose."

"O.K. 'By, Grebel. See you in the bad place."

I ran from the booth, hopped into the car, and made a screeching U turn across the tracks, then took the back streets till I reached McClintock Street. The gun was loaded with sudden death, and my heart was pumping buckets of blood and chemicals through my tense body. I parked a block away and walked in the shadows toward the house.

There was no cement on the driveway; I circled the lone car and tiptoed up the dirt to the dining-room window. I peeked in through a half-inch shaft of light that came out through a torn curtain. I could barely make out the cruel, blunt features of the two thugs. They frightened me. They were the real stuff, and knew how to do their jobs. Then a third one walked in; he was worse than the others and showed his teeth, said something funny, and felt low on his body. All three of them laughed and one of them made an international gesture and said something. I cursed silently and brought out my gun.

There's a certain awareness that we've carried over from prehistoric days. Common sense told me that nothing was behind me; they were all inside. But I dropped to my knees and swung my gun fist hard as I pivoted around. I felt it crack into a dark shape that loomed over me like a bad dream. The body fell and started to scream. His gun fell out of a suddenly limp hand, and I brought mine up and smacked where I hoped a face would be.

There was a sound of cracking bone that resembled nothing in this world, then a gurgle of hatred, and the body lunged forward. I aimed at the face that fell toward mine and swung again. There was a grunt, blood sprayed on my face, then there was silence, a whole nightful of it.

I threw myself on the huddled shape, raised the gun, and drove it into the face beneath me, not once, but forever. Finally I stopped and leaned back, looking down at the dead man who would have no face in the grave. It was nothing more than a pulpy mass, a bowl of mashed avocados with a bare seed for the nose. I tried to pull the head up, but it collapsed in my hands, the skull bones making little scraping sounds.

I turned away in the bushes and threw up.

God, I was sick!

I wiped my mouth across my sleeve, cleaned the bloody butt of the gun on the grass, and dragged the dead man out of sight. Through the window, I could see only two men now. One was playing solitaire and the other was watching him silently, half facing me and idly playing with some cartridges that lay in an open box. I walked around the house and onto the wooden steps of the back porch.

They creaked beneath my weight, and my heart was pounding madly when my hand reached forward to open the screen door. I stepped inside and felt my way through the blackness, then turned a corner and entered the kitchen. To the left, from under a door, a crack of light showed. I froze and watched it; from the dining room, I could hear the low voices of two of the thugs. Then a toilet flushed, and I stepped quickly next to the door. The light flashed off just as the door opened. Wormlike, I tried to work my way into the woodwork of the wall and stood, the gun held in my upraised hand like a blackjack. The man turned his face toward me, then away, and started to do a double take. The gun swung silently down, jarring my arm clear to the shoulder. I caught him as he moaned and crumpled.

I eased him to the floor and sapped him again, feeling the gun break through his skull and hearing it squish just a little as it sank into the brain. He stopped moaning. Then I opened the door that led from the kitchen and stepped into a hallway, walking noisily, bravely, as if I had guts to spare.

I held the gun waist high as I made my way toward the middle of the hall where the light shone out. I walked and stood in the door, and the gun was an impartial judge as it studied the two men. They were sitting at a round dining-room table, bare and scarred with cigarette burns.

They looked up, and their startled faces gave me all the time I needed. I shot the first one through the head; his skull and hair rose magically. I snarled and turned to the other one as the noise and blast of the gun, the smell in the room and the power I received from the recoil took me away from Los Angeles and threw me back to the Po Valley.

I swung the gun toward the other one. He had risen, and his hand was pawing inside his coat when I said:

"Hell's waitin'! Good-by!" at the same instant that I fired.

The first shot threw him back into the chair. The second one caught him in his throat and ripped out the back of his head. I guess it did, because there were little pieces of bone on the window shade like flys trapped on flypaper.

I looked down at his feet and saw them twitch for several seconds. I guess they were getting nervous while they waited for Charon and the ferry ride across the Styx. I walked to the table, picked up the half-empty box of .38 slugs, took the gun from the second one's pocket, and ran through the dark house up the stairs, taking them three at a time.

I was a madman as I ran through the second floor into every room, switching on the lights, then dying a little when I found each one empty. A small flight of stairs led to the attic, and I made the closed door in four leaps. It was locked, but the key was on the outside. I unlocked the door and flung it open, felt blindly for the light switch, then squinted in the suddenly too bright room.

Doris was on the bed, tied hand and foot, her eyes watching me.

I untied her, mumbling things that didn't make any sense. She didn't speak, just looked at me. I held her close, then her arms went about my neck and she started shaking.

I grabbed her shoulders and shook hard. "There's no time for that, Doris. We've got to get out of here—police any minute. Let's run!"

She tried to, but her legs were rubber bands. By the time we made the front door, they had improved a little, and I pulled her into the night. Three solid citizens had gathered in front of the house and were gawking inside. I held Doris by the arm, urging her to hurry, and swung my gun toward them.

"Get the hell away if you want to live!" I screamed.

The maggots slithered back into the safety and darkness, and I dragged Doris toward the car. A minute later, I shoved her inside and got under the wheel. Just as I started to turn on the lights, a prowl car with its red light blinking screeched into McClintock. I pulled Doris down out of sight and waited till the whirring car passed us. It turned into the driveway and came to a slamming halt.

Two of L.A.'s Finest jumped out and ran into the house. I turned on the ignition and softly pulled away from the curb. Two people pointed and started running toward the car. I mentally gave them an obscene gesture and rocketed away from the death house on McClintock.

CHAPTER EIGHTEEN

"I HEARD the shots, and I prayed, Jack."

"I don't blame you. I'd have prayed, too."

"No, I prayed that it wasn't you. I didn't want you hurt."

The traffic signal turned red, and as I waited for half a minute, I turned to her. "Do you love me, still?"

"What do you think?"

"I think that I love you, too."

She didn't say anything till we turned west on Santa Barbara. "Did you kill them?"

"Yes. Did they hurt you?"

"One of them tried, but he didn't."

"The bastard! I hope he died hard." I remembered the first man that I had killed that evening and swallowed back the sickness.

"Where are we going, Jack?"

"I'm taking you away."

"No!" she cried. "I want to be with you!"

"I'm boss here. Now, let's have some quiet while I think."

I recalled the motel where the kids had been making gay love the night that I tumbled into their lives. It would be as good a place as any. The owners would know what we came for, but for five dollars, they wouldn't care. So no baggage? So what?

I went to a service station, washed my face after nearly throwing up at the sight, then went to the motel. She clung to me, trembling violently.

"I won't let you go till you tell me what you're going to do!"

"Look, baby, it's a one-man fight from here on. I've got a hunch that I'll be winding up tonight at Moss's house on Sunset. But you guess with me."

She pleaded and stormed till I told her where I was keeping Manny and Mardi. I gave her Grebel's address, then Moss's, so that she could feel as if she were in the mess, protecting me. Then I asked her:

"Are you afraid to stay here?"

"No, Jack," she said quietly.

I reached inside my coat pocket, suddenly conscious of the weight. I picked out another .38 and placed it on the table by the bed. "In case anyone comes here, baby, you know what to do. I don't mean the cops, but … Hell, give it to me, you won't be needing it!"

She put her hand on my arm. "I'd feel safer, Jack," she whispered.

"All right. Now I've got just one thing to say, and let's not have any tears. If anything should go wrong, I want you to just disappear. Does anyone know your name?"

"No. I never told them."

"Good. Then go up to your folks in Santa Barbara. Promise?"

She nodded. "I promise."

"Fine. Good-by, Doris. Sorry I got you in this."

"I wouldn't have had it any other way, Jack. Good-by."

I drove away, leaving her standing in the middle of the room, dry-eyed, her hands stiffly held at her sides. Suddenly, even though I was sick of the whole thing, I wanted to meet Grebel. I didn't want to die, because life was a precious thing to hold to. Funny, when you read about Mr. So-and-So's death, you mentally shrug and pass on to the comic section. And when you die, someone else will shrug and start reading the want ads so he can get a better job so someone else can …

Yike!

I pulled up to the curb on Bunker Hill and slowly walked up the stairs, dog tired. I rapped on Manny's door and talked briefly with Flossie's leg man, then went back to see Mardi. She was awake, sitting on a cane-bottomed chair. I was willing to bet that her little glamour bottom had criss-cross marks etched into it by then. For some reason I didn't want to find out.

Flossie saw me enter and sat up in bed. She had tied strings to each of Mardi's bound arms, carrying them on to her bare toe, making a very neat alarm system. She rubbed her sleepy eyes.

"Hi, lover, what's the latest? Gawd, you're a mess! What's that on your shirt, catsup? As if I didn't know," she ended, shuddering.

"I'm afraid to look. It's blood." I turned to Mardi. "I killed them with your husband's own little thirty-eight." She shuddered and looked away. "Ain't it hell?" I asked, my teeth showing, but not much humor.

Her face whitened, but she didn't speak, just looked at me again, her face expressionless. I turned back to Flossie, who had disconnected the strings and was putting on her shoes.

"Did you get a story from her, Flossie *mia*?"

"From that thing?" She spat invisibly on the floor. "As far as she's concerned, I'm not living. She reminds me of one of those ham actors who don't want to talk to the lousy reporters till their so-called careers are flying out the window. Nope, she won't talk."

"Pay it no heed, news hawk. You'll get your story if I have to die helping you." My body shook a little and begged me not to talk that way.

I sat on the bed and talked quietly to Flossie, telling her everything that had happened, except where I had hidden Doris. She didn't bother to take notes; her mental recorder got it all. Then I walked back to Mardi.

"Better talk now, Beautiful Dreamer. Time's flitting underneath our feet, as old Omar said, and pretty soon you'll be talking to a jury of your peers. Remember, the papers can help oodles. They can mean the difference between a light stretch at Tehachapi and a quick onceover in the gas chamber."

Mardi shook her pretty head, and her innocent eyes belonged on the Mona Lisa. "You've changed, Jack."

"Sure, why not?" I grinned. "I don't get a double cross like this in every lifetime. Wouldn't *you* change, Doll Face?"

"You were so—so …"

"Search for the word, honey. What's wrong with 'nice'? Let's write a song, 'Nice Enough to Sell Out.'" I cupped her chin in my hand. "I was very nutty about you once, Mardi."

Her voice was soft, personal, sensual. "Could you be again, Jack?"

Her lips parted, as if they were waiting for my kiss, and her eyes searched mine, taking me back to that first night. They were so sincere that I could have believed them with no trouble.

Flossie's tenseness reached across the room to me, and her breath drew in as she waited for my reply. I bent down, my lips less than an inch from Mardi's. Her mouth waited. Her teeth gleamed, her breasts tried to reach out to me, and her arms were twitching, waiting to snare me forever. Her tongue slid from her mouth, wet her lips, and retreated, waiting just inside for mine.

"No! Not in a million years!"

Mardi sank back in the chair. Her eyes closed, and I stood watching her sag into a pitiful blob. I felt sorry for her; I've always felt sorry for anyone who passes up the humble first love of another person. Then I remembered something and spoke to her again.

"Grebel beat you up that night, didn't he? It wasn't Moss, after all."

She nodded, started to speak, then shook her head slowly.

"You didn't want to go through with it. For just a little while you felt sorry for me. Why?"

She looked up, and her eyes were wet. Her voice was soft, and I barely heard her answer. "I loved you, Jack. But it was too late.

Now!" she screamed. "Get out of here! I can't—" She broke down, sobbing, her head dropping to her breasts and shaking slowly.

I jerked my head at Flossie. "C'mon outside."

We left the door ajar so we could watch Mardi. Flossie put her hands on my shoulders.

"I'm proud of you, Jack. I was wondering."

"Maybe I was too, but when she asked me, it wasn't hard."

"No harder than pulling a couple of teeth, maybe?"

I nodded and lit two cigarettes. "Something like that."

"What's next?"

"I'm damned if I know for sure. So much has happened that I've got to let my thoughts catch up with my actions. I guess I'm going after Grebel now."

She shook her head. "You're pushing your luck too far. He'll know by now that the thugs are dead, and he'll be looking all over town for you. Oh, my God!" she cried, smacking her head with her hand.

"What's the matter?"

"Grebel probably knows that I called Manny, and he's going to connect me with you. If he finds out about this place, look out, brother."

"Do many people know about it?"

"No, but—"

"Don't start getting the jitters. That's what makes people old."

"*Not* getting the jitters sometimes doesn't let them get old, too. Well ..."

"Yeah. Forget it for a while."

We talked some more, but words don't mean much when all that remains is action. We ground out the cigarettes on the floor and finally Flossie said:

"I hate to ask you this, but where are you going to get proof—the grand-jury type, I mean?"

"I wish to God I knew." I jerked my head toward Mardi. "She's got it, she told me she did, and she's kept it a secret. I believe her, because she's just smart enough to hedge her bets. But she won't talk, and I can't work her over any more. She's a woman, and there's no way I can fight her."

Flossie's face got tight. "Leave here, go buy a beer, and come back in an hour. We'll see!"

"No, I won't let you."

"Oh," she breathed. "Going soft on her after all?"

"No—never again!"

"All right, then. Listen. Don't forget that you're not the only one wrapped up in this mess. I'm in it, and so is my leg man. I've been figuring back. He and I have compounded felonies by the bucketful—unless we can prove that you're innocent. Then we're heroes. But right now we're accessories after the fact to murder, kidnaping, harboring a fugitive, and God knows what else that you haven't told us about. Maybe the Mann Act, for all I know."

I tried to say something, but her hand waved me quiet. "We're both in quicksand up to our necks, and we've got a right to pull ourselves out. Do you honestly think that I came into this mess for a story and nothing else? Sure, I'll take it, write it up, and maybe win the Pulitzer Prize, but that wasn't the real reason.

"I hate these dirty thugs that prey on little people like you and me. That's the real reason I'm here next to you right now. That first day I talked with you, I realized that lots of things were at stake, more than just your life, or mine. Something big was up, a matter that affected everyone in the country if you want to carry it that far. What about all the people who are victimized by the rackets? I've got a right to get the proof, fair means or otherwise. These people are riding too high. Kefauver helped a little bit, but the people are forgetting again. Now, we've got to wake them up with something so damned strong that they'll *never* go back to sleep.

"I'm mad now, goddamned mad, and I know what to do with that bitch in there. I know what they're proud of, what they couldn't stand to lose even above death. When I get through with her, believe me, she'll talk!"

I looked into her narrowed eyes, down at her tight hands, thought back over the past weeks, then said, "Go to work on her!"

I looked at Mardi. She had been listening, and her head drooped forward again. Flossie smiled grimly.

"Come back in an hour."

I rapped at Manny's room and went in when the leg man opened the door. Manny was sleeping fitfully, and occasionally his fat body jerked, the layers of fat billowing like waves on a turbulent sea. His mouth opened and closed grimly as one dream progressed into another. I turned back to the leg man.

"How's he making out?"

He pointed toward a quart milk bottle. "I never thought I'd turn into a nurse, but … What the heck, it's all in a day's work."

"That's right. Thanks for everything you did. That took guts."

He grinned. "Maybe a little bit of Flossie's windmill-charging nature has finally rubbed off on me."

"How about taking some time off?"

"I could stand some chow."

"Flossie's Olds is downstairs. Why don't you run out and get some? I'll watch Sleeping Beauty."

"O.K., thanks. I'll be back soon."

After he left, I sat and looked down at Manny's tortured face. He had gone into the throes of a nightmare, probably dreaming about falling eyes first into a needle factory. I smoked through several cigarettes, then shrugged and sank back. Another sound came, muffled, and I heard a soft cry. Then there was silence, and I could imagine Flossie whetting a butcher knife on a stone.

For more than an hour I waited till a soft knock sounded on the door. I let Flossie's boy friend in, took two hamburgers that he had thoughtfully bought for Flossie, and left the room.

For a half hour more I waited in the hall, squatting on my haunches, unconscious of my aching legs. Mardi was crying almost constantly. A cloth ripped and Flossie said something that made me cram my fist to my mouth. And then Mardi's low voice started, haltingly at first, then ran into itself in its eagerness, and Flossie tramped to the door. The light shot out into my wet eyes, and she stuck her face out at me.

"Come on in. She'll talk now."

Flossie walked back, panting, and sank on the bed, covering her head in her hands and bending forward as if she felt sick. Mardi was a mess, something you would dig up from one of the worst graves. Her breasts were heaving.

Her face was bloodstained, her eyes were in hell, and there was a long gash on her thigh.

I should have felt sorry for her. But I didn't.

I straddled a chair in front of her, but her eyes wouldn't meet mine till I snapped, "All right, let's have it. The whole story!"

She looked up at me. The glaring bulb that hung over her cast harsh shadows, all black and white with no in-betweens, and made her look old, haglike. She tried to shake the hair from her eyes, but failed, and I took my hand and smoothed it back over her head. As my hand passed her cheek, she turned and kissed it. I drew it back as if it had been burned. She saw the gesture and smiled a little.

"Come on, quit the stalling," I growled. "Start at the beginning."

She started to talk, robot-like, as if she had known the words from her birth. For more than an hour she spoke, talking constantly and without prodding. She probably didn't realize it, but the things she said would start a chain reaction, commencing beneath the hallowed foundations of City Hall, "He that violates his oath ..." and continuing to the outlying districts, branching out and multiplying like exploding firecrackers till they at last reached the state capitol, and eventually Washington, D.C.

And then her monologue was finished, and it was question-and-answer time.

"Why did you marry Moss? Was it your idea?"

She shook her head. "Grebel thought of it. He had evidence on me, enough to put me in jail. We met when he was on the Vice Squad, and I..." She trailed off.

"Go on, beat the bushes. At this late date you can't afford to be coy."

"I—had been running a house." Her face lifted eagerly to mine. "I wasn't working in it, really I wasn't, Jack..."

I interrupted her. "You just sold the bodies at so much a pound. I'm proud of you!" I sneered. "So then he made you marry Moss?"

"Yes." Her head fell forward.

"Next week, 'East Lynn.' I'm crying for you, so don't think you don't have a friend." I lit a cigarette. "Don't feed me that stuff, save it for the birds. We all know that if you were running a house, you had to have protection. There's only one trouble with you. You're a congenital liar. Where did you meet Moss?"

"At one of his clubs on the Strip. He liked me."

"And Grebel was in the game even then, wasn't he?" She nodded. "And visions like sugar plums danced through your head, and you and Grebel sat down and talked it over and worked up a neat little foolproof racket—nearly. You married Moss and started riding higher and higher, and Grebel followed you right on up, because you supplied him with information."

"Yes, but—he made me do it."

"You poor little doll!" I turned to Flossie. "Lovely romance, huh?"

"Yeah," she said dryly. "It'll go down in storybooks and take its place right along with 'Romeo and Juliet.'"

Mardi bit her lip hard. "Jack, what are you going to do with me?"

"I'm not sure yet, and I know what *you're* going to do if you expect to get out of this mess with your little pink hide all in one piece. You're going to give me all, and I mean *all,* of Moss's records that you copied."

Her face whitened. "Grebel would kill me!"

"Maybe so, but you're going to do it. Want to know why? Because if you don't, you're going to be sacked away for murder."

"Murder!"

"That's right. You're as deep in this as the others. Now, where are the papers?"

"I can't tell you."

I turned to Flossie. "I thought you had our little canary all primed and ready to sing."

Flossie shrugged.

"All right for now, Mardi. We'll go back to that later. Maybe right after Manny talks. Then you're going to be glad to spill whatever you know." I turned back to Flossie. "Did you get anything from Manny?"

"Nope. You made a true believer out of him, and he won't confess his sins to anyone else."

I rubbed my hands together. "Let's go in there now. All three of us!" I untied Mardi and walked her down the hall.

Mardi licked her lips, shoved me away, and made a dash for the front stairs. But her legs weren't working very well, and I caught her with no trouble. After the attempt, she collapsed. Her head fell on my shoulder, and I had to pick her up and carry her to Manny's room.

I stood her up against the wall. Inside, Manny was awakening. It was nearly dawn. Through the front windows, the distant hills were gray, flat-looking like painted scenes on a stage canvas. My mouth tasted bad, and my brain was groggy. I walked over to Manny. His eyes had been following me around the room, and for the first time he saw his girl buddy.

"Mardi!" he croaked.

"That's right, Manny," I said. "And do you know the other lady? She's a good friend of mine."

"I know the bitch. Sow-belly Narbonne!" he snarled.

Flossie calmly took off her high-heeled shoe and limped crookedly over to Manny, a terrible smile on her face. If I hadn't grabbed her arm just as she raised it high and aimed, she would have put a spiked heel through his skull. She growled angrily at me, tossed two four-letter, hyphenated words at Manny, leaned against the wall, and put her shoe back on.

I lit a cigarette, looked with interest down at Manny's hairy chest, and finally said, "Manny, how about telling Miss Narbonne why you killed Moss?"

"Are you nuts?" he snorted.

I sighed. "Well, here we go again, huh, Manny? Where the hell did I put those needles?"

His face tightened, then he got brave with the women in the room. "You wouldn't have the guts. It's all a bluff."

"Bluff? Tell yourself that when you're reading the story of this case in Braille." I turned to the leg man. "Got a pencil and paper?" He nodded and fished out a notebook and chewed-up pencil. "Put them on the bed next to Manny, will you?"

I leaned down over Manny. "Now, Manny boy, you're going to write a full confession. This time I'll really have to work you over; there isn't too much time left. I may end up by breaking every bone in your body, except your writing arm. So you can make it hard on yourself, or easy. Really, I don't care. I hate you, and it'll be pure joy to work on you."

"I wish to God I had you down like this, Griffith!"

"Are you going to talk?"

"No!"

"Flossie, do you want to leave the room?"

"Who, me? Heck, no. This I gotta see. Go to work, and when you get worn out, I'll take over. I know lots of tricks, too.

Have you ever heard of the water treatment? We've got a fire hose out in the hall. You take the hose and tie Manny on the bed ..."

Manny gasped, and I untied him. "The door's unlocked, Manny. All you have to do is get by me. Do that, and you're a free man."

He sat upright on the bed, rubbing his arms, then closed his eyes for a second. At first I felt sorry for him. He was a worn-out, empty husk. But then I changed my mind.

He lowered his head and charged me. His head slammed me in the stomach, and I rolled to the floor. He raised his foot and kicked at my jaw; I rolled to one side and jumped up. He lowered his head again and charged. I stepped aside and let him have one over the ear. He staggered, swung around, and fell to the floor. I picked him up and led him back to the bed.

Then I went to work on him.

Thirty minutes later, he was crying.

Ten minutes after that, he was jibbering. Several times, Flossie had gulped, and the leg man's face was a grayish color, but his hypnotized eyes never left the bed. Mardi turned her face away and retched, her body torn by dry heaving.

Manny fainted. I walked over and got his quart bottle, filled it from the cold-water tap, and sprinkled it in his face. While I waited, I looked out of the window. I couldn't bear to look at their faces. When he came out of it, he saw my face and started crying again. I bent down and whispered something to him, then reached into my pocket. But before I could bring out a knife, he whispered something in a voice so low that I had to strain to hear it.

"I'll write!"

For nearly half an hour he wrote, stopping now and then to sniffle and raise his pained eyes to mine. I read the paper over, then tied him to the bed again. He was so used to it that he held his arms in place for me. I had Flossie and the leg man witness the paper, and Flossie read it, her eyes gloatingly happy. Everything was tied up into a neat little package.

All but one thing. Grebel.

Manny hadn't really implicated Grebel any more than a smart lawyer couldn't un-implicate. I needed one more thing, the pay-off papers. I walked to Mardi where she half lay in the middle of the room and knelt down.

"Where are the papers, Mardi? The little game's about over, and you'd better get on the right team."

She was silent.

"Where are they?"

At first I thought she was holding out, but when I turned her face toward me, her eyes were blank. I repeated the question slowly three more times, shaking her gently. Then she said:

"In my home—bedroom."

"The copies you made?"

"Yes."

Manny tried to break loose from the bed when he heard her admit it. His voice snapped across the room. "Dirty bitch!" he screamed. "Ya held out on me! Your friend!"

She pushed herself up from the floor and walked slowly toward Manny. She stopped above him. "Friend!" she cried. "You don't have a friend!" I felt like laughing. Then in the next breath, when she spat in his face, I felt a little like crying. I turned to Flossie.

"I'm going now."

"For God's sake, be careful. Do you want any help?"

I folded the roughly written confession in my pocket. "Uh-uh. You all stay here."

I looked toward the leg man, who was standing idly by the window, looking down on the street below. Suddenly he stiffened and wheeled about. His face was tight, and his mouth was sagging open.

"Police! They're coming in, Grebel and another one."

"God Almighty!" Flossie prayed.

Mardi turned around to see me, her eyes lit up like twin candles. Her face twisted, and her snarling lips moved silently before she could speak. Then she said:

"You son-of-a-bitch! Now we'll see!"

CHAPTER NINETEEN

I STOOD for long seconds, staring at Mardi, barely hearing her screams. I looked at the leg man and over to Flossie.

"Is there a back way out?" I quietly asked Flossie.

"There isn't any fire escape in back. You'll have to jump from the window onto a tin shed. You might make it."

"Let's go!"

"No!" Flossie spat. "There isn't time. For God's sake, beat it! You're our only chance. And if you *do* get away, call the real cops. I'd rather be arrested than murdered."

I turned to the leg man. "Do you want to go with me?"

His lips got tight. "I'll stay here—with the ladies."

"All right. Sorry I got you into it."

"Get moving!" Flossie screamed.

I wheeled from the room and barely made the far end of the hall when cautious footsteps started up the stairs. I shoved the window up and almost fainted at the twenty foot drop below. Then all thoughts left my mind. I climbed to the ledge and pushed myself out into space. I hit the slanting tin roof with a ringing thud. My knees slammed down, and I started rolling. At the edge, I swung around, grabbed the overhanging eaves, and dropped another fifteen feet to the ground.

My teeth jarred together and my stomach felt as if it had almost torn loose from its moorings. For less than a second I stood there, then ran diagonally to the tall board fence that separated the alley from the front street. It made an army obstacle course look infantile. I jumped up, my fingers curled around the top, and I pulled myself up, my kicking shoes urging me on. I poised for an instant, then dropped to the cement sidewalk.

The sounds from my leather soles echoed ahead of me, but there was no stopping. The twenty-five or thirty feet that lay between me and the street lengthened themselves out, nightmare-like, and I seemed to be running in molasses. Above me, a window shot up. Grebel yelled, and I looked up. A gun trained itself on me for an instant, then blasted. The noise was terrific in the narrow passageway. My ears ached, and in the same second my body cringed for the impact.

I got it in the left shoulder. The shock threw me to the ground, and I rolled out of sight next to the house. I pushed myself up and ran around the corner to the street. My shoulder was numb.

As I ran, my trembling fingers searched my pocket for the ignition key. I slid into the car and made the slot in one jab. The car was bumper to bumper with the police car in front, and after I started the motor, three life-killing seconds passed before I could back up. I slammed the car into reverse and backed up, slid it into forward gear, and hit the gas hard.

The engine died.

It was the death angel, not a snarling plain-clothes cop, that ran down the stairs, gun drawn, aiming at me. I bent low, jammed the starter button, and heard the engine take hold. I slid down just as a gun blasted. One slug ripped through the window and out the other side. The other buried itself in the upholstery next to me.

Without even seeing where I was going, I slammed the car in gear again and screeched from the curb, cutting the wheels hard to the left. The right fender of the car smacked into the police car; I was thrown against the steering wheel, and my teeth bit through my lip. My car rocked and swayed, then, with a rending sound, tore itself loose and rocketed away.

Just before I turned north on Flower Street, I looked in the rear-view mirror. The cop jumped in the car, let loose with a blood-chilling blast on the siren, and burned rubber as he took off after me. Traffic cleared before me. I turned west and nearly died when I saw the pavement suddenly disappear as a nearly vertical hill dropped in front of me.

I took a deep breath and kept my foot on the throttle. I flashed down the hill, ran through a red stop signal, and sped beneath an overpass. My foot tramped harder on the accelerator, and in my mind fleeting pictures of the last week passed through my mind, each one opened by Mardi and closed by Doris. I ran through four more stop signals. Heads gawked and stared.

I forgot the dip west of Alvarado till I was on top of it. I grabbed Fate's dice and kept my foot on the gas. I bent low over the steering wheel and tried to aim the wheels straight at an imaginary point on the horizon. The car smacked the dip, took off like a gazelle, then hit the pavement nose down. The front bumper scraped and the tires screeched as they fought to keep traction.

But Old Man Fate was smiling down on me when the car hit, its nose pointed straight ahead. I started breathing again and looked into the mirror just as the chasing car hit the same dip. Its front wheels were turned only a fraction of an inch, but that was enough. It dipped and flew up at least three feet, came down sideways, smacked the black asphalt, and started rolling. From a block away I heard the rending, ripping, and scraping. It hit the curbing, vaulted over it, and smacked into a store front.

The last thing I saw were flames slowly rolling from the car, a hand reach up vainly and fall back, then people running toward the wreck.

I slowed down and felt sick.

How much can you take? After a while you get so you really don't care what happens. Things lose meaning, and you want to curl up and forget about everything but dying. But I couldn't afford the luxury of dying yet.

Here we go again, Jack. Hold tight!

I called the police station, told them that Jack Griffith was holed up at Flossie's place, assured them that it wasn't a gag, and hung up. Then I headed out Sunset Boulevard.

Moss's home—not his present expensive cement-vaulted copper coffin, but his previous one—was what they call an English colonial. It had once looked proud, but now, as I sat in the car and looked at it, it was dead. Its curtains were drawn, and it lacked the vitality it once possessed through Moss's presence. I ripped into the wide drive and grated up the gravel, drove around the house, and parked in back.

My shoulder was starting to pain me, and I held it gently as I half stumbled around the house and walked into the patio that lay off the study where Moss had died.

Weeds were already beginning to grow, and the flowers were dying, along with the trampled bushes. The draperies were across the lead-paned French windows. I raised the butt of the gun and smashed the glass, reached inside, and opened the door with my left hand.

Blood had seeped into my coat, and I felt it, looked at it on my fingers, and rubbed it on my pants. The paneled study smelled like death: closed rooms, genteel regards, wilting flowers, a bloodstain on the carpet, a man with bowed shoulders looking down at the death scene, a misspent life, days too soon gone. Futility.

And cabbages and kings. And if the sea is boiling hot, and whether pigs have wings.

I walked around the room slowly, holding my aching shoulder. For no reason at all, I opened a cupboard. I saw a full bottle of Bacardi rum. I ripped off the revenue stamp, uncorked the bottle, and drank hard. The stuff burned my lips gently; I swirled it in my mouth, then swallowed. I turned on my heel and left the room, trotted up the stairs, and smacked my lips, still hanging on to the bottle.

I tromped around upstairs till I located her room. There wasn't any doubt when I opened the door. It was thickly carpeted and the walls were papered with flowers; roses intertwined, getting ready to make love and produce new hybrids. There was a chaise longue at the far side, next to an expensive television set. To the right was a small dressing table holding several bottles of cologne and perfume. The powder case was still open, as if Mardi had just finished powdering her nose and was going down below to greet the mourners.

The canopied bed was what you knew a glamour queen like Mardi would choose. The canopy was a soft, white something that draped around the bed and almost hid the coverlet.

I twitched as the shoulder burned, then ripped the canopy off, ground it beneath my feet, and turned the mattress over. I got a nail file from the dressing table and went to work on the seams. Ten minutes later the bed was a mess, and I knew that the stuff wasn't there.

The closet was next. I. Magnin could have set up a clearance sale for all of Beverly Hills with the clothes that neatly hung there, swaying gently when I entered. I jerked everything from the hangers and went through every seam and pocket. The suitcases were next, and I spilled the tender memories on the floor, pictures of her and Moss, smiling, kissing, eating, and drinking. All honeymoon stuff.

I turned from the closet and walked toward the bureau, looking at the little electric clock that hummed its way through expensive minutes. First drawer, small, meaningless, nothing-to-offer papers, a bankbook and this and that, a grubby little file. Second drawer, handkerchiefs and scarves. Lord, she had hundreds of them. Third drawer, panties, black and beige, pink and panting, brassieres and slips. Fourth drawer, neatly folded nightgowns.

Each article flew behind me as I examined it, and by the time I had finished, the clock had whirred through eight more minutes. The place was a shambles, dead looking, like my hopes for life. I picked up the bottle of rum and sank down on the chaise longue. I uncorked the bottle, held it between my legs while I lit a cigarette for a chaser, then flopped back, tilted the bottle, and felt the rum gurgle into my mouth.

For the first time I raised my eyes to the wall and saw a painting of Mardi. It was a beautifully done thing, and portrayed her in the garb of an ancient Egyptian princess. Her eyes had been accented just a bit, and her breasts were more full. The exquisitely lovely main feature, however, was the mouth. The lips were parted, eagerly waiting for something, probably the tossing to the crocodiles of an arrogant slave or worn-out lover.

I leaned back again and heard a tiny click. Nothing more, but from below it echoed like the sound of my doom. Grebel. There wasn't any doubt, and for long seconds I closed my eyes and nearly prayed for death. When I opened them, they sought the painting, for some reason. It was leering down, and I could have sworn that the lips moved and said, "Come away with me, forget all this. I will teach you pleasures that you have only dreamed of." But I knew they lied, for they could only give death.

I got up and went to the bathroom, turned on the cold water, and doused my head. It made me feel better, and when I shook my head without wiping it, I felt more like a man again. When I returned, I looked cautiously up at the picture. It had withdrawn into itself and seemed a little sad. I flopped down again and inspected the gun.

Showdown. You know the feeling, you're sitting in a game with the stakes 'way over your head. You've got a small pair backed up in five-card stud. Your sole remaining opponent is sitting across the table, grinning at you, maybe looking down your throat. He has called you and raised your bet. You call him. Your mouth has never been drier, and your heart is pounding. He slowly turns over his hole card, deliberately making you wait. You try to smile, but you can't.

For the next sweating ten minutes there was no other sound. Then, God help me, I remembered that I had not locked the door.

My heart thumped leadenly in my chest, and I tried to breathe, but had forgotten how. When I stared at the closed, unlocked door, I tried to get up. But the grating pain of my shoulder held me pinned down. My teeth were manly and refused to let me cry out, cursed at me and made me try again. I walked slowly to the door, gun in right hand, eyes on the knob.

Then it slowly and silently turned.

My eyes bugged out, and my right trigger finger clamped down; the gun rocked back in my hand and shots crashed through the virgin whiteness of the wood, making great, black holes. A surprised curse came from the upper hallway, and footsteps jumped away. I tried a grin; it was weak, but better than nothing. I reached forward and locked the door.

Grebel said just one word, but all the hatred of a dirty, crooked cop swept in it, making me feel as if I were already on trial.

"Griffith!"

I lit a cigarette. My head bobbed, trying to get in step with my jerking fingers. I inhaled deeply and coughed like a kid learning to smoke. I tried again, and was successful, then blew the smoke out, saw it flatten against the door, and search for the bullet holes. I grinned. I felt good and laughed aloud for the first time in many days. I yelled, "Grebel!"

"Griffith, you don't stand a chance. The whole force is coming over here!"

"You're a liar, Grebel. You know damned well you can't afford to have the whole force in on your secrets. Guess why? Because, as Mardi probably told you, she hid an extra set of papers here in her bedroom. And I found 'em, you son-of-a-bitch. I've got 'em right here in my grubby little fist. If you want 'em, come in. I'm waiting!"

"What the hell do you mean?"

"I've got 'em all, you bastard, everything from the dope list to the pay-off roster. Yeah, and your name heads it and ends it."

"You've got nothing on me!" he roared.

"Wait and see, or better yet, come in and look for yourself. Shoot the lock off, kill me, then see your name. It reads better than the funny papers. But, brother, I've got one thing to tell you. When you come in, come in shooting, because you're not going to get them while I'm alive. I've got too much at stake, and when I get out of here, I'm going to talk. Lord, how I'm going to talk!"

"O.K., Griffith, you asked for it!"

"*I* asked for it!" I screamed. "I didn't ask for anything except to be let alone. I wasn't bothering anybody, but you and that woman you call your wife framed me. It's curtains, Grebel. The end's in sight!"

Three shots ripped out and splintered the door. I jumped farther to one side, suddenly glad that he had fired the gun; he knew fear also. I went back across the room and started constructing a fort. I turned the dressing table over, sending several bottles of perfume onto the thick carpet. The chair was next; it fitted on top of the table. I picked up the chaise longue for my rear-echelon reinforcements and laid it on its side.

I left enough room between their sensually curved legs for the ugly snout of my gun. The cigarette in my lips had burned itself down, and I enjoyed grinding it into the deep carpet. My fingers started fumbling with the box of shells. They fell to the floor, but my eyes didn't follow them, because I had seen something.

There, securely taped to the bottom of the chaise longue, was a bulging envelope, and there wasn't any doubt as to what it was. I tossed the gun to the floor and ripped the envelope open. For the next minutes, I all but forgot Grebel as I studied the evidence.

There it was, everything for the people of the state of California. The smart lawyers couldn't talk their clients out of this tight jam. I felt sick when I recognized the names of popular movie and political figures as having been in on the dirty rackets.

A shot ripped into the lock, then another.

I picked up the gun.

CHAPTER TWENTY

THE DOOR CRASHED OPEN, leaving a great hulk in its place. The gun slammed against my palm three times, and Grebel fired rapidly till his own gun clicked emptily, then he jumped out of sight. I should have aimed better, but when death is brushing its wings against your face, you don't always think.

Over my loud panting, I could hear Grebel breathing slowly and surely, like a powerful bull getting ready to charge its enemy. I spilled a few reloads into my pocket and dumped the rest on the floor, broke the gun apart, and reloaded. I clicked it back in place and waited, heard Grebel's gun snap back, then listened to nothing but silence, the sort that drives you mad with anxiety. What's he going to do next? you ask yourself, at the same time knowing that there's no way of finding out till he decides to do it.

And still the door gaped open, a subtle invitation to death. For some reason fear had left me and was replaced by cold hatred. Now that the moment was at hand, I could have faced them all. The gun in my sweating palm had turned me into a superman.

I lit another cigarette, then held my fingers out at arm's length. I was proud of the way they stayed extended as if they had been cast from plaster of Paris. The smoke gushed into my lungs; the odors of tobacco and burned powder mingled with the spilled perfume and made the room smell like a den of vice.

"What are you waiting for, Grebel—guts?"

Silence.

My finger kept constant pressure on the trigger, and if a fly had buzzed through the door, I would have dropped him on the wing.

My forehead started sweating. The cigarette was growing a long ash, and I jerked my lips, letting the ash fall onto my coat. Some of it dropped onto the drying blood and clung there. I grimaced and turned back to the death watch.

"O.K., Grebel, play hard to get. I can wait you out."

I took a perfume bottle from the floor and could smell its fragrance even over the cloying aromas in the room. I tossed it toward the door. It slid across the carpet into the hallway, stopping just short of the railing.

"There's some of Mardi's sweet smell, Grebel," I called. "I wonder how many times Moss has licked it off her shoulders? Hey, buddy, have you ever been in her bedroom? It's really pretty. I guess Moss liked it, too."

A hand snaked around the door and fired blindly. I ducked low, then peered through my fort openings. "What's the matter?" I laughed. "Nervous in the service?" More silence. "I've got a deal for you, Grebel."

After a long silence he spoke. "I'm listening."

"If you drop dead right now, I promise to give you the best little old funeral you ever had. I'll dance on your grave and let Mardi lean on my shoulder. Then she and I will come back here, pull the covers down, and—"

"You funny son-of-a-bitch!" he screamed. His arm snaked around the door again, and his finger clamped down twice, the twin blasts nearly deafening me. My own gun rocked three times, making splintered nicks where his arm had been. Two shots ricocheted off into the house, and somewhere below a window tinkled. Then there was silence, big bundles of it.

The next armistice dragged into long minutes, and my nerves wore thin. I wondered how Grebel felt.

I jerked my gun back to the door just as Grebel roared and leaped inside the room. He saw me an instant after I squeezed down on the trigger. His gun flew up, and he fired. My gun blasted again, making one sound with his, and if I hadn't seen the little flame surge from his, I wouldn't have known that he fired.

If I hadn't got the slug in my guts.

I fell to the floor and continued firing, my remaining bullets tracing a mad pattern up his body. Then the gun was empty, and I lay looking at it stupidly. He stood over me, part of his jaw shot away. The gun was at his side, and he raised it.

But it weighed tons, and he was having trouble. He got it hip high, and I said to my body, This is it!

He grabbed it in both hands, and it trembled upward, weaving like a fluttering bird. But he didn't quite make it. He rolled to one side and tried to grin as he fell forward on me. I felt the crushing impact of his body, then it rolled off and was a piece of beef that a slaughterhouse wouldn't have given two bits for. His blank face was dug into the carpet. The little pulsations of blood finally stopped, and his body twitched once more.

But I knew that he was dead before then. You can tell.

I pushed myself erect and staggered from the room. I felt my way along the hall, leaning against the railing. At the top of the stairway, I stood looking down. Then my knees gave way and I slumped down.

I crawled down the stairs and found my way to the study door. I clawed it open and blindly felt my way to the desk.

I pushed up on my knees and grabbed. My fingers caught the cord and yanked. The phone fell to the floor beside me. I leaned against the desk, cradled the receiver behind my ear, and dialed the operator.

Before the blackness swirled over me, I got three words out. "Griffith—Moss Morrison's house."

Then there was no more.

Except the hospital and courtroom, foggy remembrances of events, faces and scowls, thundering denunciations about the "mad killer," and my own attorney's staccato replies.

They threw the book at Mardi and Manny, then turned to me and did their level best, but I managed to dodge all but a few of the pages. But by then I didn't care, because at last the whole mess was over.

And then suddenly Doris was in my arms. "I'll be waiting, Jack."

"Forever?"

"Maybe even a little longer."

"I'll be back. We've got a heap of living to do."

"A heap of living," she whispered.

I started to speak again, but never made it, because her lips were silencing mine with a kiss that took away all words.

She would be there—always.

THE END

www.ingramcontent.com/pod-product-compliance
Lightning Source LLC
Chambersburg PA
CBHW020121180626
46812CB00006B/2682